OUT OF LINE

OUT OF LINE

a novel

Jen McLaughlin

The author acknowledges the copyrighted or trademarked status and trademark owners of the following wordmarks mentioned in this work of fiction: Coke, University of California San Diego, Girls Gone Wild, Marines, TMZ, Hollister, Glock, M-16, iPhone, Motrin, Swarovski, Converse, Harley Davidson, Discovery Channel, Islands, McDonald's, The Hangover, Conan, Apple, Wonder Woman, Richter Scale, and Pepto-Bismol.

Edited by: Hollie Westring at hollietheeditor.com

Cover Designed by: Sarah Hansen at © OkayCreations.net

Interior Design and Formatting by: E.M. Tippetts Book Designs

This book goes out to Caisey Quinn, my wonderful critique partner.

Without you threatening my life if I didn't finish this book…it wouldn't be here.

Desperate to break free…

I've spent my entire life under my father's thumb, but now I'm finally free to make my own choices. When my roommate dragged me to my first college party, I met Finn Coram and my life turned inside out. He knows how to break the rules and is everything I never knew I wanted. A Marine by day and surfer by night, he pushes me away even as our attraction brings us closer. Now I am finally free to do whatever I want. I know what I want. I choose Finn.

Trying to play by the rules…

I always follow orders. My job, my life, depends on it. I thought this job would be easy, all the rules were made crystal clear, but when I met Carrie Wallington, everything got muddy. She's a rule I know I shouldn't break, but damn if I don't inch closer to the breaking point each time I see her. I'm ready to step out of line. And even worse? I'm living a lie. They say the truth will set you free, but in my case…

The truth will cost me everything.

Trying to resist…

Her lips parted to let out a little moan, and I swooped in, entwining my tongue with hers. She gasped, almost as if she'd never been kissed before, and then melted against me. She wrapped her arms around me, urging me even closer, and my hands fell to her hips. Unable to help myself, I pressed my cock against the soft curve of the side of her ass, reveling in the feel of her softness pressed against my hardness.

Fuck, I wanted her.

Tearing my mouth free, I took a ragged breath and held her still. She kept trying to wiggle in my lap. If she kept that up, this would be more than a cover kiss. It would be a cover fuck. I tightened my fists on her and opened my eyes. She did the same, looking back at me with smoldering blue eyes.

Well, that answered my question from earlier.

Her swollen red lips begged to be kissed some more, but I tamped down the urge. I had to remember the game. Stay on course. "Shit. I shouldn't have done that. Pretend it never happened."

She blinked at me, the heat fading from her eyes and being replaced by confusion. "Why?"

OUT OF LINE

CHAPTER ONE

Carrie

I leaned against the wall and surveyed the crowded room. All around me, people were in pursuit of the three majors of college: getting drunk, getting laid, and then getting even drunker. They were shouting in each other's ears to be heard over the deafening music, sucking on each other's body parts, or throwing up in a corner. The overachievers would do all three by the time the night ended.

It was freshman year at its finest—and I was the only freshman not fitting in.

But at least no one had been *paid* to hang out with me at this party. When I was twelve, my father had thrown me a huge birthday party. The turnout had been particularly surprising to me, considering the people who came were the same girls who told me what a loser I was while in school. Of course, as soon as my parents left the room to get cake, the girls had backed me in a corner and pulled at my hair and dress. They had told me that I was such a loser my father had to pay their parents to make them come. Susie had gotten an iPod. Mary received a phone. Chrissie—a pony.

I had gotten a cold, hard dose of reality.

A tall guy bumped into me, hauling me out of memory lane. His beer tipped and spilled all over my open-toed sandals. The cool liquid was almost a welcome change from the stifling hotness.

"Oh, shit. I'm sorry." He dropped to his knees and started patting at my feet with the closest object he could get his hands on. It looked like a shirt. "I wasn't watching where I was going."

I laughed and shook my head, dropping a hand on his shoulder. He felt a tiny bit sweaty, but who could blame him? It was freaking hot. "Don't worry about it. Seriously."

"No, it's not." He lifted his head and his eyes went wide. "Oh, fuck. Do I know you?"

My smile slipped a little bit, but I forced it back into place. He wouldn't recognize me. I had been out of the public eye for well over a year, and I'd made sure to change my appearance quite a bit. I also had much longer hair, and my body finally grew into itself. My braces were gone, and I outgrew those god-awful bangs, too. I liked to think I didn't look anything like the gawky girl I'd once been.

Please, God.

"No, I don't think so. But don't worry about my feet. It's not a big deal. I was just leaving anyway."

He stood up. "Are you sure?"

"Positive." I smiled at him, hoping my sincerity showed. "Thank you, though."

He gave me one more smile and headed back toward the bar. I watched him go before I worked my way across the room. I needed to get out and breathe some fresh air. Somehow I even managed to make it through the crush without spilling my Coke. As I pushed through the door, the ocean breeze washed over me, immediately calming my pounding heart.

One thing I hadn't managed to change about myself in my big transformation: I still didn't do well in crowds. I never should have listened to my new roommate, Marie. I had only been at the University of California in San Diego for two days and had already been invited to four parties. I'd turned down all but this one. It wasn't because I was a prude or anything. I just didn't like the craziness that parties entailed.

After all, I had ultimately picked this campus because the occupational therapy program was excellent—not because of the parties. It also had the added bonus of being on the beach *and* as far away from my parents as I could possibly manage without leaving the country. They were great, and I loved them, but man, they liked to smother me. The "hold me down kicking and screaming as I tried to break free" type of smothering.

That was the last thing I needed at this point in my life. I needed to try to be on my own. To try to make my own place in the world. And for once I was really, truly on my own…outside of a raging party that I didn't belong in, hiding in dark shadows that hid only God knew what.

But still. Awesome.

I kicked off my sandals and trudged down the sandy hill to the dark beach, sinking my toes into the chilly sand. Probably not the best combination with the beer bath I had just taken, but whatever. My mom and dad had never let me walk barefoot in the sand. It was too unclean, and syringes might be buried deep down—plus other unmentionable items Mom blushed just thinking about. She couldn't even say the word *condom* for cripes sake.

I was convinced I must have been conceived via subliminal messaging or something. My parents were far too proper to do the down and nasty. Too proper to walk barefoot on a dark, scary beach. And I was supposed to be the same. Grinning, I dug in even deeper, loving the way the sand felt between my toes.

I scanned the shadows and found a bench a few feet away. When I sat down, I swung both of my bare feet in the air and let out a deep sigh. There was probably a homeless guy sleeping a few feet away from me in the darkness, but I didn't give a hoot. I was alone, in front of the ocean, listening to the waves crash on the sand.

For the first time since coming here, I felt at peace. Maybe I could fit in. There had to be some people here who were like me—a little bit dorky and a lot awkward. The door opened behind me, and the sound of heels clacking on the pavement interrupted my thoughts. "Carrie? Are you out here?"

"Yeah. Over here," I called out.

"Are you trying to get mugged?"

"No. Just trying to find a homeless guy to fall in love with," I replied, keeping my voice light. "So far, no one wants me."

"Whatever," Marie said, snorting. After a few moments, she stood in front of me, heels in hand and hands on hips. Marie frowned at me from behind a veil of perfectly arranged blonde hair, which blew in the ocean breeze. "You totally bailed on me."

3

I flinched. Yeah. I kind of had. "Sorry. In my defense, I did tell you parties aren't my thing."

"That's something girls say when they don't want to seem like sluts." Marie waved a hand and shoved her hair out of her face. Within seconds, it was back. "I didn't think you actually *meant* it meant it."

"Well, I did." I swung my legs some more, trying to distract myself from the righteous anger being thrown my way. "You can go back in. I just needed some air."

"Will you be back?"

"Maybe." I blew out a breath. "No."

Marie's light blue eyes pierced into me. "Are you going to be like this all year long? I like you and all, but you're kinda lame."

"I'll try not to be," I said as honestly as I possibly could. Because I *would* try to be sociable and outgoing and not so lame. I would probably fail. "But it will be a while till I'm there."

Marie rolled her eyes and fluffed her hair with her hand. "Well, hurry up. I'm not going to be lame with you as you struggle to adulthood."

"You don't *have* to do anything. Go back to the party." I shooed her away, a smile on my face. "I kind of want to be alone with my homeless boyfriend."

Marie eyed me, the hesitation clear in her eyes and the way she held her weight on one foot, the other slightly lifted. "Are you sure?"

"More positive than a proton."

"Oh my God. Never say that again."

I laughed. "Fine. Now go have fun."

"Okay." Marie hugged me tight, and her hair tickled my nose. "But next time, you stay whether or not you want to. Enough lameness."

I watched her go. We were complete opposites, but maybe it would make us great roommates. Marie might be the person to pull me out of my self-imposed shell, and I could make sure Marie studied as hard as she partied. It had the makings of a win-win situation. Maybe. Of course, it could be a complete and utter disaster too.

But I was trying to be optimistic, thank you very much.

I leaned back against the park bench, letting out another sigh. I would sit here for another minute before I headed back to my room. Once I got there, I'd curl up with a good romance book with my current book boyfriend and pretend the real world didn't exist for a little while.

It would be the perfect Saturday night…for a sixty-year-old woman.

Lame, lame, lame.

After a couple of seconds of pure relaxation, I stiffened. Someone moved in the shadows. I almost missed it, but out of the corner of my eye I caught movement. Who was out here with me? If Dad were here, he'd be saying it was a druggie desperate for his next hit. He'd sic his private security team on whoever dared to walk near him. I used to go back to the spot and give whoever had been held back by my father's team some money. One of Dad's security officers would go with me.

But I wasn't my father, and I refused to jump to the worst conclusions. I stood up and crept toward the shadows, my heart in my throat and my legs feeling less than steady. My mind screamed at me to turn around and run home, but I ignored it.

"H-Hello?" I called out, but it sounded more like a croak than a word. I licked my lips and swallowed hard, taking another step toward the ocean. "Is anyone there?"

Nothing but the waves crashing. I hesitated. Someone was there. I knew it. "I know you're out there. You might as well come out. If you don't, I'll…I'll call the cops."

I held my breath, waiting to see if the hidden person would call my bluff and come out. After a few seconds, a shadowed form stepped forward. As the shadow grew closer, I realized it was a man. A guy who stood at least six feet tall and had muscles that I thought only existed in the romance books I read.

He had to be a couple years older than me, maybe a senior, and he had on a pair of cargo shorts and nothing else. Hot damn, he obviously worked out. A lot. He had short, curly brown hair, and he looked harmless enough. But those muscles…

Okay, when I goaded the guy out of hiding, I hadn't been expecting a freaking bodybuilder to walk out of the shadows. I backed up a step, biting down on my lower lip. "Who are you, and why are you hiding in the shadows?"

He had a black tattoo of some sort on his flexed bicep. Wait. Scratch that. He had tattoos pretty much from his elbows up and all across his shoulders and pecs. Hot. *Really* hot. This was the type of guy Dad kept me away from. He had bad boy written all over him. In numerous ways.

He rubbed the back of his neck and stepped closer, towering over me. "Who are you, and why are *you* hiding in shadows?"

I blinked and forced my eyes away from his ink. "I wasn't. I was sitting on the bench."

"Maybe I was too, before you came out." He grinned at me. "Maybe you stole my seat."

"Did I?"

"Maybe."

I shook my head and tried not to smile, but it was hard. For some reason, I liked this guy. "You like that word, don't you?" I held my hand up when he opened his mouth to answer. "Let me guess. Maybe?"

He laughed, loud and clear. I liked the sound of it. "Perhaps."

"Oh my God, he says something else." I held a hand to my forehead. "I might be imagining things."

"Hm. You *do* look a little flushed."

Probably because an off-the-radar hot guy was talking to me. Maybe even flirting? Crap. I had no idea. The last time a normal boy had flirted with me, Dad had his security team drag him out of the mall by both arms. I had no doubt this guy would get the same treatment if he ever crossed paths with Dad. "I do?"

He stepped closer and bent down, his eyes at level with mine. They were blue. Really, really blue, with little specks of darker blue around the pupil. People were always telling me that I had the prettiest blue eyes in the world. They were wrong. This guy did.

"Yep. Definitely flushed."

I cleared my throat and tucked my hair behind my ear. Until I remembered it was in a ponytail. Then I ended up kind of rubbing against my ear, trying to make it look like I'd *meant* to do that. And probably failing miserably. "I'm fine."

"I didn't say you weren't." He backed off and smoothed his brown hair, but it bounced right back into perfect disarray. He headed for the bench I had been sitting on and lowered himself onto it. "So, tell me. Why are you outside instead of partying inside?"

I followed him, scooted my shoes between us to maintain a safe distance apart, and then sat down on the edge of the bench. "Uh...I needed some fresh air. And this party is a little bit too crazy for my tastes. The frat boys are a little crazy too."

He nodded. "So, you new here?"

"Yeah. I'm a freshman." After smoothing the stupid skirt Marie had conned me into wearing, I looked at him. "Do you go here?"

"Yeah, I'm a senior." He cocked his head toward the house. "And I'm in that frat."

"Oh." I looked down at my lap. So I'd insulted his friends. Great. Just great. "I'm sure it's a lot of fun."

He grinned. "Even though they're crazy?"

"Uh, sure." I smiled back at him, but inwardly flinched. It was too late to tell him that the guys were perfectly normal. I was broken—not them. But I would look even more like an idiot than I already did if I told him I'd left because of my own lameness. "Maybe I'll give it another chance."

He chuckled. "Not tonight, though, right?"

"Nope. Not tonight." I played with the hem of my skirt. "I'm all partied out. I drank too much."

He looked at my cup. "You better watch yourself. A lot of guys will take advantage of a girl who drank too much."

"But not you?"

His eyes darkened, but he looked away. "Not me."

It was a pity. I'd never been taken advantage of by anyone, but if I was going to be used, I'd prefer he be the one doing it. I kind of snort-giggled at the thought, earning a weird look from him. Oh well. He wasn't exactly the first person to shoot me that look. "Then I guess I'm in good company."

He shrugged. "You should go home and sleep it off."

"It's only eleven," I argued. I conveniently ignored the fact that I'd been planning on going home mere moments before. That had been before *him*. "Why would I go to bed already?"

He looked at me, running his gaze up and down my body. "You look like the type of girl who's used to playing by the rules. Good girls go to bed early."

I was, but I was also freaking sick of being that girl. All my life, Dad had neatly moved me around on his chessboard, a pawn to his own plans. I was done being a pawn. I wanted to be the queen of my own life from now on.

Leaning in, I caught his gaze. He stiffened, a light shining in his eyes I didn't fully comprehend. "Maybe I'm the type of girl who's sick of living by the rules and who's ready to have some fun."

CHAPTER TWO

Finn

When she leaned in close to me like that, I gripped my thighs. I felt ridiculously out of place right now. I was in a pair of board shorts, pretending to be a carefree surfer dude so that my overprotective, needs-therapy boss could "rest easily" while his perfectly capable daughter attended college. I didn't even have my *gun* on me. And to top it off? Carrie was a cute little thing who was looking at me as if she wanted nothing more than to crawl all over me.

I needed to get close to her, but not *that* close. Even if I wanted to.

Her soft red hair reminded me of Scarlett Johansson as Black Widow. I had always had a thing for her—what kind of hot-blooded American man hadn't at one point or another? I especially liked her when she carried a kick-ass gun and wore black spandex and boots. It wasn't a far stretch of my imagination to picture Carrie in Scarlett's getup. Her short skirt left little to the imagination, and I wanted her. Bad.

I'd never had such an instant attraction to someone before. The type that demanded I find a way to get her in my arms, naked and writhing, before the end of the month, but I couldn't have her. I forced myself to picture Senator Wallington's face instead of Carrie's. That should help. "I think you look like a good girl who wants to try her hand at being a bad girl."

"Maybe." She shrugged. "But maybe not. You don't know anything about me."

Ah, but I did. I had her file memorized. And I'd been watching her from the shadows all night long. I also knew enough about her to know she hadn't been drinking tonight. Knew enough to know the real reason she wasn't inside was because she hated crowds. She hadn't been to any real parties until now. And I knew her father was controlling enough to send an undercover agent to watch his nineteen-year-old daughter fumble her way through freshman year.

One thing I knew about repressed girls who went away to college: They went all *Girls Gone Wild* on crack as soon as they got even the slightest taste of freedom.

The girl was looking for trouble with a capital T. Even I could see that.

She licked her plump, red lips and met my eyes. "So, you going to your room or staying out here with me?"

Oh yeah. Trouble indeed. I shifted in my seat. The girl had no idea what kind of attention she was welcoming. She might only be a couple of years younger than me, but even so, she had *off limits* stamped across her forehead. I forced a lighthearted laugh. Something I suspected a California boy would do. Hell, something *I'd* once done. "I don't really live here. I was fucking with you."

"Oh." Her brow furrowed. "Which dorm do you live in?"

"None." I grinned at her, even though my cheeks hurt from smiling so damned much. "I don't even go here. I'm just a surfer who lives nearby. Can't afford the fancy education."

That much had once been true, at least. When I'd been eighteen, I couldn't afford the tuition. That's why I had enlisted in the Marines. My plan had been to use the GI Bill to earn my degree, but I hadn't gotten to that point in my life yet. As it was, I had shadowed my father's footsteps and joined the Marine reserves fresh outta high school. I had been ooh-rah'ing it for five years now and had attained the rank of sergeant. On top of that, I held the title of "assistant private security officer" with the senator's security team.

I could afford to go to college now, but I was too busy. And now I was here in California. I'd been picked for this assignment since, as the youngest employee at twenty-three, I was the most likely candidate to blend into a college campus.

And if I managed to keep Carrie out of trouble, I would return to work minus the "assistant" in my title—and a spike in my pay. But first I had to get close enough to her to be able to be in her company, but not so close that she wanted me even *closer*.

"Oh, I totally get that," she said, nodding as if she had a clue about what it was like to be poor. She didn't.

Her daddy could afford to buy this whole campus without blinking. Hell, he'd already made a *sizable contribution* to get the dean to allow an undercover agent to linger around campus and follow a student. "Yeah?"

"Yeah." She plucked at her skirt again, her shoulders hunched. "I mean, not personally, but I know how bad the economy is right now. I'm not some bimbo college student. I watch the news."

Sure she did. Maybe TMZ was her version of "news," but it sure as hell wasn't mine. "I'm sure you do, Ginger."

She gave me a look. I could tell she wasn't sure if I was insulting her. Maybe she had more brains in her pretty head than I gave her credit for. "My name's not Ginger."

I gave her a cocky grin. "I think it has a nice ring to it, though. Don't you?"

"No," she said flatly. "So if you aren't going to college, what do you do?"

"I'm a Marine," I said. "And the rest of the time I surf."

I tugged at my Hollister cargo shorts. Apparently that's what all the California kids wore nowadays. I must've grown up since I left, because I preferred wearing a suit with a Glock or a pair of cammies…with a badass M-16.

"Nice. I'd like to learn how to surf sometime. It looks so freeing."

I cocked a brow. What an odd choice of words. "Freeing?"

"Yeah." She stole a quick look at me, her cheeks pink. "Like…it's just you and the ocean, and no one can tell you what to do or how to act. No one can yell at you for riding a wave, or just sitting out there, watching the world pass by. I don't even really know how that feels, and I doubt I ever will."

With a father like hers? Doubtful.

I'd resented being asked to come here to babysit some spoiled little brat, but seeing her look so despondent tugged at the little bit of heartstrings I had. "I'll teach you, if you want."

Fuck. Why had I opened my stupid mouth and blurted out that shit?

"Really?" She perked up, her shoulders straight and her sapphire blue eyes shining. She looked way too pretty right now. Way too much like a pretty woman, and not enough like an *assignment*. "Do you mean it?"

Hell no. "Sure. Why not?"

I could think of at least a hundred reasons why not. The last thing I needed was to spend time with her out in the ocean. She'd probably wear a tiny bikini underneath her wetsuit. And she'd cling to me in fear, her slender body pressed to mine as she learned how to ride the waves…

Maybe she would chicken out and say no.

"Can we start now?" she asked, practically shouting in my ear. She hopped off the bench and did a little dance thing that was way too fucking cute. Her whole body trembled with excitement. I could *feel* it rolling off her. "I'm game if you are."

I choked on a laugh. So much for her chickening out. Some small part of me admired her enthusiasm. A lot of girls wavered and couldn't make up their minds. I was getting the sinking suspicion she wasn't that kind of girl. "I think we should do it when we can actually see what we're doing."

"Tomorrow morning?"

I scratched my head and scrunched my nose. "Uh, you'll need a board, a bathing suit, and a wetsuit first."

"I have a bathing suit already." She cocked her head. "Wait. Does a bikini work, or does it have to be a one-piece?"

It was on the tip of my tongue to say she needed a one-piece. At least it would cover more of her skin, but she might find out I lied, and then she would start to question everything I told her. I couldn't afford that right now. "Bikinis are fine. Preferred, even."

She nibbled on her lower lip. "Would you go shopping with me tomorrow? Help me pick out the right gear? Then maybe we could head out to the waves."

Shopping? Hell no. I didn't want to go shopping. For girls, shopping was a marathon sport. I'd probably be dragged through ten stores before she could find the perfect color surfboard. And a matching wetsuit. And probably a fucking hair bow, too. "I'd *love* to."

I forced a smile and tried to look on the bright side of things. I needed to spend time with her, and this would accomplish that. After the heinous shopping experience, I would be rewarded with surfing. It wouldn't be so bad, would it?

"Thank you." Her cheeks flushed and she gave me a shy smile. "Where should we meet?"

"At your dorm around eight?" I met her eyes. "Or is that too early for you, Ginger?"

She stiffened, the fetching pink color leaving her cheeks. That was probably a good thing, since she looked far too cute wearing a blush. There was that steely determination again. When she looked at me, her eyes flashing with challenge, she looked like her father. "I'll be there. I don't sleep in till twelve."

"All right." I inclined my head. "Then off to bed you go."

She laughed. "You can't send me to bed. Who do you think you are? My father?"

Hell no. But I worked for her father, so that had to count for something. "Hey, if you want to surf, you need to be well rested. If you're hung over and tired, I'm not taking you."

"I won't be hung over."

I eyed her cup, even though I knew damn well it didn't have alcohol in it. "Tell that to the judge."

"Fine. I'm going to bed." She clamped her mouth and grabbed her shoes. "I'll see you in the morning."

"I'll walk you," I offered, standing up. It would make me feel better to know she was safely ensconced behind locked doors before I went back to my apartment. It *was* my job, after all.

She flushed and ducked her head. "If you want to. But you can't come in."

She was probably thinking I wanted to walk her home to try to steal a kiss or cop a feel. Well, she could think that all she wanted. It wasn't happening. In fact, it had been strictly forbidden. I had even gotten a lecture from the senator about what was allowed and what wasn't—complete with a signed contract. As if I was a child who needed to be shown on a fucking doll where I could and couldn't touch.

I shoved my hands in my pockets, feeling ridiculous. "I wasn't planning on it."

"Then why walk with me?" she asked, her head cocked.

"So I'll know where to meet you tomorrow." I shrugged. "Ya know, for our shopping."

"Oh. Right." She started walking, and I fell into step beside her while scanning the shadows for any threats. "I knew that."

I laughed lightly. "Sure you did."

"I can't think of any other reason you'd want to walk me."

I shook my head, then realized, like an idiot, I'd never asked her what her name was. If I accidentally blurted it out before she told me who she was, the gig would be up before I even got started. "What's your name, anyway?"

"Carrie. Yours?"

She left off her last name just as her father instructed her to do. I could report back that she was following instructions like a good little girl. Although…walking with strange men she met on the beach after dark wasn't exactly playing by the rules. But since it was with me, I would let the infraction slide this time.

"I'm Finn. Finn Coram."

She gave me another smile. She looked so pretty, smiling at me in the moonlight. It would be a hell of a long year keeping the horny college boys off her. "Nice to meet you, Finn."

"Back atcha, *Carrie*," I said, forcing a grin. I hated acting like a foolish boy. Hated pretending to be something I wasn't. "But I still prefer Ginger."

She hesitated, licking her lips. "Can I ask you something?"

"Sure. Go for it."

"Why are you teaching me how to surf? What made you offer?" She stole a quick glance at me. "Why are you being so nice to me?"

Already, she was questioning my motives. My respect for her grew. This wasn't a bimbo socialite. She knew to use caution, even if she wasn't using enough of it. I shrugged. "Why not?"

"In my world, there's always a reason." She lifted a shoulder and stopped at a pathway leading to a big dorm. "So you've got to have one."

"Yeah, well, I don't." I leaned against the building next to hers and crossed my ankles. "This your building?"

She didn't answer my question, but narrowed her eyes on me. "I'll meet you out here at eight."

"All right."

She stared at me. I arched my brow in return, waiting to see what the hell she was waiting for. If it was a good night kiss, she would be waiting a hell of a long time. She tapped her foot. "You can go now," she said.

"I'll wait until you're safely inside."

Her foot stopped tapping and she glowered at me. Oh, yeah. She definitely took after her father. "And *I'll* wait till you leave."

We stared each other down, neither one of use seeming to want to be the one who looked away first. After a bit more of our little Mexican standoff, I chuckled. "I can do this all night, Ginger."

"So can I." She tilted her head and studied her nails. "You know, you're starting to remind me of my father's private security firm."

"Your father has private security? Or he works in it?"

She flushed. "Yeah, he has security."

"Why?"

"None of your business. Is there something you want to tell me?"

"Of course not." I laughed but shifted on my feet. She was way too close to the truth already. I would need to back down to remain undercover. "Do I *look* like private security?"

She ran her gaze over me. "Not really, but that doesn't mean anything. You're being awfully…protective."

"Ya know, I'm a Marine. It's kind of our thing to guard people."

She pursed her lips. "Fair enough, but still. Go *home* before I call security on your butt."

"There you go, bossing me around again." I picked up a piece of her hair without intending to do so. It was so soft and pretty. "Fine, but I'll see you right here in the morning."

"Okay." She nodded and bit her lower lip. "Bye."

I dropped her hair and headed back toward the beach, where I could then hop on my motorcycle and ride back to my empty apartment. As I turned the corner, I stopped and peeked out. She headed toward her building, her head low and her steps unhurried. I pulled out my iPhone and jotted off a quick text to update the senator.

I'm here and have seen her. All is well.

As I slid the phone into my pocket without awaiting a reply, I watched her go with a smile on my face. The senator had obviously underestimated his daughter's street smarts. Sure, she'd made a few blunders, but she'd also made some smart choices. She hadn't given me her full name, and she'd lied to me to hide her true location in case I was some creepy stalker.

Her father would be proud.

CHAPTER THREE

Carrie

With only ten minutes to spare, I hurriedly applied the last touches to my lip gloss, checked out my hair, and turned off the bathroom light. If I had primped right, I looked effortlessly, naturally beautiful. That's what the website said I would look like, anyway. I had never really bothered to primp for a boy, so I'd had to rely on my best friend for help.

Google.

Was it pathetic that I had no one else to ask? Sure. But at least Google never let me down. It had also given me *the talk*, the same one my mother avoided until right before I left for school. And when I'd finally been given *the talk*, it had been with so many euphemisms even I had become confused while trying to figure out what drumsticks had to do with warm apple pie.

I smoothed my tank top over my stomach. I had paired it with some yoga pants, and I wore my red bikini underneath the simple outfit just in case Finn wanted to go out in the water afterward. Tiptoeing past a snoring Marie, I managed to make it out of the dorm without waking her up.

I probably worried for nothing. I doubted a stampede of elephants would have woken Marie up. The girl had been snoring loud enough to wake the dead. Her arms were flung out to her sides, and a huge puddle of drool gathered under her cheek. She'd probably have a hell of a hangover when she woke up, so I had set my bottle of Motrin next to her bed on my way out.

I glanced at my phone and walked faster. A quick call home would be a good idea. That way I wouldn't have to deal with my parents while out with Finn. I quickly dialed home and leaned against the wall. They picked up on the first ring, as if they'd been hovering by the phone waiting for me to call all morning.

"Hello?" Mom said.

A line clicked as Dad picked up the phone in his office. "Carrie?"

I smiled. "Hi, guys."

"How's college going?" Mom asked, her voice trembling.

"Have you met anyone nice yet?" Dad asked.

"Yeah." I pictured Finn and smiled. "A couple of people."

"What are their names?" Dad asked. I could picture him sitting at his desk, pencil in hand, waiting to look into anyone who dared say hello to me. "I'll do a background check."

"Dad. No."

"But—"

"*No.*"

Mom sighed. "Let her be, dear."

"Fine." I heard something slam down. "But if you get involved with someone, I'll expect to get his name from you."

"She's not going to do that yet." Mom paused. "Right? We had our little talk. Do we need to have another one?"

I flinched. "God, no." I cleared my throat. "I mean, uh, no, thank you. I'm good. And I'm not seeing anyone yet. I've only been here two days."

Dad laughed. "That's my girl."

I peeked at the time. I had less than one minute to get downstairs. "I'm about to go out with a friend of mine, though. Shopping."

"Oh, how delightful." Mom, of course, perked up at the word *shopping*. "Where are you going? What are you shopping for?"

"Do you need more money?" Dad threw in. "I can transfer more to your account."

"No, I'm fine. And I'm shopping for..." I pictured the dead silence that would come if I said what I was really shopping for. It would be amusing for two-point-two seconds...until all hell broke loose. "I'm just shopping for fun. Hanging out and stuff."

"But what for?" Mom asked.

Geez. Enough with the details already. "I think swimsuits and beach gear."

"Oh, how fun."

Dad yawned. "This is my cue to say goodbye. I've got meetings all day long."

"Yeah, I have to go." I gripped the phone tight. "I love you guys."

"We love you, too," Mom said.

Dad mumbled something that might have been *I love you*, but he never said it, so it was doubtful. "Bye."

"Bye, dear."

I hung up and headed outside. I needed to get down to the meeting point before Finn did, or he would see me come out of the correct building. He didn't need to know where I lived. Didn't need to know anything about me…yet. If he proved trustworthy, then I would tell him more. Little by little. But for now, I was just a girl who liked sitting on benches at night.

A girl who wanted to surf.

It was probably the one place private security couldn't follow me. It's not like a bunch of men in suits would blend in out there in the great big sea. As I crossed the lawn, I glanced around. No one lurked in the bushes. No one suspicious followed me. I didn't believe my father gave in to my request to go to college minus a bodyguard, but I hadn't *seen* any yet.

Was it possible he had trusted me enough to be on my own? Doubtful. When I had gone abroad last year, it had been with not one, not two, but *three* security guards. He was ridiculous when it came to my safety. He'd probably installed a GPS tracking system under my skin when I was a kid. I wouldn't put it past him.

I rounded the corner and saw Finn standing there, facing the other way and looking as sexy as I remembered. I had thought he was gorgeous last night. Holy freaking bananas. In the morning light, his sun-kissed skin glinted and highlighted his hard muscles. Muscles covered in tats that begged to be stroked…by my hands. With his brown hair in as much disarray as it had been last night, he quite easily emanated the surfer look he wore so well.

Oh, so well.

As I approached, he smiled at me. "You're two minutes late, but you look pretty enough that I'll let it slide."

My heart sped up at his backhanded compliment, but I refused to show it. I shrugged and said, "A girl's gotta primp. Get used to it, Marine."

"Especially girls like you?"

I stiffened. That sounded an awful lot like an insult. And even worse, it sounded as if he knew something about me that I didn't want him to know. Did he know who I was? "What the hell is that supposed to mean?"

"Nothing." He straightened, looking less like a laid-back surfer and more like a man. A man I didn't know at all. Maybe this had been a bad idea. "You just look like the type of girl who likes to spend hours getting ready before she walks outside to get the mail. I mean, you're gorgeous. Just look at you."

"And you look like the type of guy who makes presumptuous assumptions about other people, while keeping your own nose firmly pointed in the air." I marched past him. "Forget it. I'll learn how to surf with someone else."

He grasped my elbow as I passed, his touch burning me and yet somehow sending a shiver through my veins. "I'm sorry," he said, his voice soft. "I shouldn't make assumptions. You're right."

"Damn right I am." I tossed my hair over my shoulder and glared at him. Turns out, this close, his eyes were even bluer. Really, really blue. "Now let me go."

He dropped his hand immediately and dragged it through his curls. "Can we start over? I get cranky before my coffee and say stupid things to beautiful women I'm supposed to be flirting with."

My lips twitched. Truth was, so did I. Well, the first part, anyway. I usually didn't bother to hit on pretty girls since I didn't swing that way. "Okay. Coffee, then shopping?"

"Deal." He motioned me forward as he walked beside me.

"Where will we shop?" I asked.

"At a store? I hear that's where most people do it."

I laughed lightly and stopped at the coffee booth. "You're weird."

"Aren't we all in our own way?"

"Yeah, I guess so." I nudged him with my elbow. God, he was solid. "But you're weirder than most."

He let me order my mocha latte before he stepped forward to order a plain black coffee. As I reached into my pocket to grab some cash for my portion of the order, he handed the barista his card. "I got you."

A warm flush spread through my body. No one ever paid for me. The few people I had hung out with in school had always been relying on me for purchases, but no one here knew how much money I had. No one knew my father was on the short list for presidential candidates. The anonymity was a refreshing change of pace. "Thank you. I'll get the next one."

He shrugged. "If I let you have a next time. You might kill me with boredom during the shopping trip."

"Haha. So funny." I grinned, then decided to get some payback for the trick he'd played on me last night. "Do you think I can find a Swarovski-encrusted surfboard? I'm willing to go in every single store in San Diego if needed."

"Oh, hell no." He shot me an incredulous look and turned a little bit green. "Please tell me you're kidding."

I blinked innocently and managed to keep a straight face. "Is that a no?"

He grabbed our coffees and handed me the bigger one. Once I took it, he shoved his sunglasses up his nose. "No. It's fucking fabulous." He shot a quick look at me. "Oops. Sorry."

"For what? Cursing?" I laughed at the absurdity of it. Who the heck apologized for cursing? "Sometimes I say *fuck* too. I'm not a little kid, you know."

He took a sip of his coffee. How did he do that? I would have burnt my tongue. "It feels like you are at times. Like you could be my little sister or something."

Sister? Ouch. Guess I knew where I stood with him. "How old *are* you?"

"Twenty-three." He looked at me. "What about you? Are you jailbait?"

"*No.*" I looked down at my cup. How much should I tell him about myself? I wanted to make friends. To be normal for once, but I couldn't be stupid. "I'm nineteen. I took a year off and went abroad before starting college."

He took another sip of coffee. "That's a good idea. It's how I would have done it, if I'd gone the college route."

I hesitated. I didn't want to overstep my boundaries and had no idea what a friend should or should not say to that. Or if we even were *friends* yet. "You still could if you wanted to. Do you want to?"

"Maybe someday, when I have time." He laughed. "Right now? I'm good in my career field."

"Well, you never know. You might decide to go officer someday."

He shot me a weird look. "Maybe."

"There's that word again."

"It's a good word, especially when life is filled with maybes." He stopped in front of a surf shop on the beach. "This would be a good place to start. I can't promise Swarovski, but there might be something pink."

"I don't do pink. It doesn't match my hair."

"Heaven forbid," he said, holding the door open for me. "We can't have that."

"Darn right we can't." I ducked into the store and took a cautious look around. Surfboards of every imaginable color lined the left wall, while wetsuits filled up the other half. In the back, a bunch of boogie boards hung on the wood wall. Maybe boogie boarding would be a safer choice. It wasn't too late to change my mind...

No. Not happening.

A blonde girl wearing a bikini underneath a transparent top stood behind the counter texting. She looked up when the bell on the door chimed, quickly assessing me before moving on to Finn—and staying there. She straightened and smoothed her hair. "Hello. Welcome to Surf's Up. What can I do for you?"

Finn smiled at her a little bit too widely, and his eyes dipped far too low to be staring at her face. Jerk. "My friend here needs a good beginner's board."

The girl looked at me again, but quickly turned back to Finn. "The blue one in the back is good for her. Perfect size."

"You think?" Finn walked over to the board in question and cocked his head. I followed Finn, but practically got shoved aside by the worker. I struggled to right myself before I went legs over head in the rack of wetsuits, but Finn caught my elbow without even looking my way. "You should watch where you're going, Ginger."

"I told you." I tried to pull free of his grip, but he didn't budge. "Stop calling me that."

Finn looked at me. "Why? It's cute."

"Says who?"

"Me." He dropped his hold on me and turned back to the employee, who'd been watching him as if he was her next meal. "So this will work for her?"

The employee moved closer to Finn, brushing up against him. And Finn, the perv, didn't move away. Of course not. He was a guy. The girl ran her fingers over the board, caressing it as if it was a person instead of an inanimate object. "Yes. The lines are smooth, and the finish flawless."

"What do you think, Ginger?"

I rolled my eyes at the nickname, but didn't bother to correct him again. No matter what I said, he would use it. "Sold. I'll take it."

Finn turned to me with wide eyes. "Really? That quick?"

"I don't care what it looks like. If you say it's good, it's good."

He tugged on his ear and looked at me as if I had sprouted two heads overnight or something. "All right. Next up? A suit."

I turned to the employee, using the no-nonsense tone Dad used when he wanted shit to get done. "I'd like a blue and white one, to match the board."

"Measurements?" The girl eyed me. "I'm guessing 32A?"

Total, petty lie. I was *not* a 32A, and it was obvious. "No, I'm—"

"34C," Finn replied, grinning. "Am I right?"

I blinked at him, taken off guard by that statement. Was it normal for a guy to know that crap? "Dude. What the heck is wrong with you? And *why* do you know that?"

"I'm kind of an expert in the frontal area." Finn grinned, and his eyes sparkled. "It's my thing."

"Obviously," I drawled, smiling.

He shrugged. I gave the rest of my measurements to the worker, and within ten minutes we were finished shopping. I carried my wetsuit and coffee, and he carried my board for me. I headed toward the ocean, so eager to hit the water I could barely stand still, and then sat down on a bench. He eyed me, but didn't sit. "That was a hell of a lot faster than I expected. I didn't even bring my board with me."

I took a sip of my coffee and watched the waves crashing on the sand. A surfer effortlessly rode one in, and a bunch more of them bobbed out in the water. They made it look so easy. So simple. I knew it was anything but. What the heck was I thinking? I couldn't do this, could I? If my father knew…

I straightened my back. The hell with that. I was going for it. The fact that my father didn't approve only made me want it more. Childish? Sure. Who cared? I was allowed a little bit of rebellion now and then. "Do you want to go to your place and get it?"

"I could, I guess." He looked over his shoulder toward the road. "Do you want to wait here for me?"

"Can't I come?"

He hesitated, shifting on his feet. "I only have a motorcycle. I'm not sure you want to ride that."

A motorcycle? Hell to the yes. Dad called bikes *donor cycles*. Told me if I ever even thought about setting foot within ten feet of one, he'd ground me for life. I wasn't ground-able anymore, was I? God, this freedom I now had was exhilarating. A girl could get used to this kind of life. "Oh, I'd love that."

"Seriously?" he asked, looking a little pale. "I'm not sure that's a good idea."

I propped my hand on my hip and stood. "Why not?"

"I only have one helmet."

"So what? I'll be fine. I trust you."

He looked up at the sky. "*You* might," he mumbled under his breath. Then he perked up. "What will we do with your board?"

"I'll have the store hold it for me."

He sighed. "I guess I'm out of arguments."

"I guess so," I said cheerily, my heart accelerating at the mere thought of climbing on a bike with Finn. "Cheer up. You're acting like my dad again."

He stiffened. "Stop saying that."

"Then stop acting like him," I said, smiling to show I was teasing him. "You better be here when I come back out, or I'll skin you alive."

I grabbed my stuff and headed toward the store. After a quick conversation with the employee, I came back out and found Finn standing there, his hands in his pockets and his shoulders hunched. I held my hand out and waited for him to take it with bated breath. I don't know why I did that. We weren't dating. We weren't even friends yet. I couldn't resist. He stared at my hand for a second, muttered something under his breath, and closed his fingers around mine. A shot of electricity skittered up my arm, making me jump slightly.

24

What the heck had that been?

His eyes darkened and something weird twisted in my belly in response. Something I was only loosely familiar with. Desire. I was a virgin, but I'd read about sex enough times to recognize the sensation. And I would bet my favorite pair of Converses that he was feeling it, too.

"Ready?" he asked, his voice deeper than usual.

"*So* ready," I said, peeking up at him through my lashes. "I've always wanted to ride one, but my dad wouldn't let me."

He perked up. "Maybe we shouldn't. You know, if your dad would be mad."

"Oh, please. I'm nineteen." I tugged him toward a Harley I could only assume was his. "I'll ride what I want to ride."

He groaned under his breath. "I bet you will." When we reached the bike, he grabbed the helmet off the handle and slid it over my head. I tried to pull back, not wanting to wear the ugly thing in front of him, but he didn't let me. "My bike. My rules. You wear the helmet."

"What about you?"

"I'll be fine." He gently slid the helmet the rest of the way down over my head, making sure to keep my hair out of my eyes as he did so. My heart did a weird little flip flop at the way he watched me, his eyes hot and his lips soft. His touch, gentle as it might seem, held a strength behind it.

"How do I look?"

"Perfect," he said lightly. Then he climbed onto the bike and looked over his shoulder at me. That look he gave me was the look that so many books described. Like he was inviting me to fall into his arms and stay there forever. God, I wanted to. His muscles flexed, teasing me with his perfection. "Climb on and hold on as tight as you can."

I swallowed hard and slid on the back of the bike.

CHAPTER FOUR

Finn

One thing I knew with picture perfect clarity? The senator was going to fucking kill me for taking his precious little girl out on a bike. Skin me alive and castrate me. Hang me up as a warning to all the other low-level security officers he employed. I would deserve every second of the pending torture, because not only did I want to take her on the back of my bike—but I also wanted to *take* her.

In several positions.

The second Carrie backed me into a corner and insisted she ride my bike with me, I'd known I was fucked…but not in the good way. Just the idea of her wrapping her pretty little arms around me and squeezing those perfect 34C's against my back made my cock hard. The reality of her pressed against me might be the death of me.

Everything I'd thought I knew about her so far had been wrong. I'd been so sure she would turn out to be this spoiled brat who thrived on shopping, drinking, and defying Daddy. Okay, the last part might be true, but she was also more. A lot more. I wanted to get to know her better. Preferably while naked in my bed.

No. My job was to serve. Protect. Keep my cover. And most of all? Not touch her. The bad thing was, I couldn't seem to stop *thinking* about it. For some reason, the little socialite who wasn't really a socialite was getting under my skin, and I had to find a way to get her out before it was too late.

If only my Glock protected against that shit.

Carrie slid onto the bike and wrapped her whole body against me. I bit back a groan and tried to ignore the way my cock was screaming for attention. Her legs wrapped around me, pressing against me. It would be so easy to turn around. To rip the helmet off her head and kiss her until she realized that the best way to get back at Daddy was through me.

But that wasn't my job.

And that wasn't me.

I didn't play the part of bad boy. Never had.

I revved the engine to life, taking my frustration out on the throttle, and she squealed and hung on even tighter. I couldn't tell if she was more excited or terrified. Probably an exhilarating mixture of both. The girl was getting a chance to live, and she obviously loved life.

Grinning, I shouted over my shoulder, "Hold on tight, Ginger."

Her nails dug into my waist and she scooted even closer, if that was possible. My grin faded away to a grunt, and I pulled away from the curb a little too hard. She didn't panic and cry out. Instead, she whooped. Actually whooped, for fuck's sake.

If she were anyone but the senator's daughter, I would be bringing her back to my place so I could show her how to *really* live. How to feel more alive than ever—and I could show her every damn night if she wanted me to. I twisted the throttle and turned the corner on the PCH, letting the bike climb up in speed slowly. Instead of clinging to me for dear life, she loosened her hold on me and laughed.

By the time we completed the short ride to my apartment, I was ready to explode with want. As I booted the kickstand into place, she hopped off of my bike and ripped the helmet off her head. Her wild red hair was a complete and utter mess, but she looked beautiful.

She did a little dance and handed me my helmet. Her blue eyes were sparkling. Vibrant. Full of life. I couldn't help but wonder what they would look like if I kissed her. Would she look up at me like that, with sapphires shining in her eyes? Or would they smolder and simmer, slowly heating me and making me need more?

"That was freaking awesome," she said, spinning in a circle. "I want to do it again and again and again."

My cock twitched, giving a whole new meaning to those words. "Anytime you want it, you let me know. I'll be at your beck and call."

"Really?" She gave me an odd look, as if she was wondering if I meant something else.

And, fuck me, I did. "Really."

"Why are you being so nice to me? It doesn't make any sense." She tucked her hair behind her ears and flushed. "I can't help but think there's a motive behind all this that you're not telling me. Are you…did someone…send you here?"

My heart twisted at the look she was giving me. All puppy-dog eyes, begging me for the truth. I wished I could give it to her. Wished I hadn't signed a contract stating I would keep my cover, no matter what.

Wished I wasn't a liar.

I hadn't expected it to be this hard. I hadn't expected her.

The girl was too smart for her own good. She was onto me. The only way to blow her off course was to confuse her. I couldn't blow my cover. Couldn't be exposed. No matter what. I grabbed her hand and yanked her sideways onto my lap. I liked the way she felt there. "You want motive? I'll give you motive."

She looked up at me, her mouth in a perfect O. Her hands fell to my shoulders, and she clung to me. "What are you—"

I slammed my mouth down on hers, telling myself the whole time that I was only kissing her because I had to keep my cover. That this wasn't *real*. Didn't mean anything. But the second her soft lips gave in to mine, I knew I was full of shit. I might be doing this to keep my cover, but I was also doing it because I wanted to see what she tasted like. To hear her little sounds of pleasure.

Her lips parted to let out a little moan, and I swooped in, entwining my tongue with hers. She gasped, almost as if she'd never been kissed before, and then melted against me. She wrapped her arms around me, urging me even closer, and my hands fell to her hips. Unable to help myself, I pressed my cock against the soft curve of the side of her ass, reveling in the feel of her softness pressed against my hardness.

Fuck, I wanted her.

Tearing my mouth free, I took a ragged breath and held her still. She kept trying to wiggle in my lap. If she kept that up, this would be more than a cover kiss. It would be a cover fuck. I tightened my fists on her and opened my eyes. She did the same, looking back at me with smoldering blue eyes.

Well, that answered my question from earlier.

Her swollen red lips begged to be kissed some more, but I tamped down the urge. I had to remember the game. Stay on course. "Shit. I shouldn't have done that. Pretend it never happened."

She blinked at me, the heat fading from her eyes and being replaced by confusion. "Why?"

"Speaking of favorite words…" I mumbled under my breath. I rubbed the back of my neck and sighed. "Was that motive enough for you?"

"Y-Yeah, I guess so." She licked her lips, her gaze on my mouth. "I didn't know…didn't realize you were thinking about kissing me. I wasn't expecting…that."

She sounded so innocent right now. Had she ever been with a man? I couldn't imagine a girl that looked like her still being a virgin…but then again, with her father, it was definitely a possibility. "Well, I'm a guy. We're always thinking about—" I broke off, swallowing the word *sex*. "Kissing. Surely you've been kissed before."

"Of course," she quickly said, her cheeks red. "Tons of times."

Tons? Why didn't I like the sound of that? "Oh really?"

"Really. You're hardly the first guy to show an interest. I'm not some meek little virgin girl."

She had to go and tell me that, didn't she? "Good to know."

I set her on her feet and stood, my heart pounding in my ears. That kiss had been a huge mistake. An even bigger mistake than accepting this assignment in the first place.

She pressed her fingers to her lips and looked at me. "So that's why you're being nice to me? Because you want to kiss me?"

"Occasionally." I forced a nonchalant shrug. She had to think I wanted her, but I couldn't actually *have* her. What a fine line I walked. One step too far to the left and I would be a goner. "I'm a guy. I'm always in the mood to kiss someone."

"Anyone will do?"

"Pretty much."

"Oh. I see." She cocked her head. "So that's your motive."

I dragged a hand through my hair and started for my door. "Sometimes there isn't a reason or a motive. Sometimes it just happens."

"Not in my life."

"Well, maybe you need a new life."

"Maybe." She bit her lower lip. "It's not that easy to just trust someone, especially when you don't even know them."

I swallowed the guilt choking me back. I knew she was suspicious, and she had every reason to be wary of me. I was a fraud. A phony. A fake. And most of all? An asshole for kissing her under false pretenses. "Why are you so damn suspicious of everyone and everything?"

She didn't follow me, but put her hands on her perfect hips. "I don't know."

"Why are you glowering at me like I drowned your kitten in front of you?"

"Because I thought we were friends."

"We are."

She lifted her chin up. "Friends don't kiss friends then say *shit*. You obviously don't like me very much, so I'm going to make this easy for you. I'm leaving—and you're staying."

"No, you're not." I rubbed my eyes. Unbelievable. Instead of fixing this screw up, I'd managed to make it worse. "I'm your ride."

She pulled out her phone and put it to her ear. "Yes. I'd like a cab, please. It's an apartment building. Brick with patios and balconies. I'll be outside." She rattled off my address, an address I didn't even know she'd be able to figure out, and then slid the phone back in her purse. "Problem solved. Now go away."

She sat down on the curb, her back to me, and promptly ignored me. I hesitated. Should I do what she wanted and go inside to come up with a plan? Or should I try to fix this now? The urge to bang my head against the wall was almost as strong as the urge to pull her into my arms was. She looked so alone sitting there and staring out in the road. I approached her slowly, uncertain how to tackle this.

"Look, I'm sorry." I sat beside her, my leg touching hers. She shot me a dirty look, but didn't move away. "I didn't mean to kiss you. Not because I don't want to, but because I just want to be friends."

"Then why did you kiss me?"

"Because I couldn't stop myself," I admitted. It was one of the most honest things I had said to her all day. "But I should have."

She finally looked at me again. "Why can't you kiss me? What's so wrong with it? I mean, if you want to, why is it bad?"

Good question. "It just is. In my career, I could be gone at any second if they call up my unit. I can't have relationships."

"That's bull." Her hands tightened on her knees. "If you don't want to be with me, just say it. Don't give me half-assed reasons why you can't."

"I don't want to be with you," I said, my voice coming out harsher than I intended. I reached out and closed my hand over hers, trying to soften the blow. "Not in that way, but I do want to be friends."

"I'll think about it." The cab pulled up and she stood. Her hand on the door, she glanced at me over her shoulder. "But if you want to be friends, keep your lips off mine from now on."

"Deal. Still want to surf?"

She hesitated. "Not today. I have a headache. See ya some other time."

And with that, she closed the door in my face and left me standing on the curb. My phone buzzed, and I pulled it out. Her father, of course. The man had impeccable timing.

Things going well?

I tightened my grip on the phone and typed fast. *I got it covered.*

Good. Don't forget the rules.

The ones I'd already broken? As if I could.

CHAPTER FIVE

Carrie

Later that night, after Finn kissed me and dissed me, so to speak, I came out of the bathroom in a pair of frog jammies and found Marie sitting on my bed, a short dress in her hands. Since Marie was already wearing a way-too-short black dress, I could only assume the tiny blue dress in Marie's hands was for someone else. That someone else better not be *me*.

I raised a brow and eyed the contraption. "What's up?"

"What's up is you're going to lose the froggies and slip into this." Marie tossed the dress at me and I reflexively caught it. "And we're going to go party. And for once in your life, you're staying."

I held the dress to my chest. "I told you, I don't like parties."

"That's because you never drink at them, I'd bet." Marie stood up and gave me a little push toward the bathroom. "But tonight, you are. I'll get you something good, and we'll party the night away. Monday classes start, so we'll have a boring week. But tonight?" She shoved me into the bathroom. "We dance!"

As the door closed in my face, I flinched. Marie might be pushy—literally—but she had a point. The week ahead of us would be long. Would it be so wrong to let loose and have some fun tonight? Look at all the other stuff I had already done since getting here.

Buying a surfboard? Check. Riding a motorcycle? Check. Kissing a hot surfer boy? Double freaking check. As long as I wasn't crazy and didn't get caught on camera naked or something, there wouldn't be any backlash. Surely Dad drank in college, right? Oh, but that was different. *He* was a man, and *I* was his baby girl.

Rolling my eyes, I sent a mental eff you out in the universe. I made quick work of shedding my froggie pajamas and slid in to the short dress. Spinning in front of the mirror, I cringed. The thing barely covered my butt. Wait. Maybe it didn't even cover it at all.

"I'm coming in," Marie called. As she opened the door and barged through, she paused. "Wow. You look amazing. All you need is makeup and we'll be ready to go."

"I don't really—"

"Wear makeup? I know." Marie pulled out an eyeshadow brush. "But tonight you're different, remember?"

Different. That sounded nice. I closed my eyes and let Marie work her magic. But when I closed my eyes, I remembered that amazing kiss Finn had given me. And then I remembered our fight afterward. He was always acting so…contradictory. It didn't make any sense. Marie started applying the eyeshadow, and I belatedly said, "Not too dark."

"I know, I know." Marie set to work, and I tried to relax. This was supposed to be fun. "Your dad called. I told him you were studying at the library."

I swallowed. "Why did you do that?"

"He calls every hour. He needs to back off. He a cop or something?"

I laughed. "No. Just overprotective."

"Ah." I felt Marie's shrug, even though my eyes were shut. "My dad was like that before he died."

"I'm sorry," I said. Dad was annoying, sure, but I couldn't picture life without him. "How long ago?"

"Two years." Marie closed the mascara, and seemed to close the topic. "Open your eyes now."

I refused to look at myself yet. I was scared I would look more hooker than sexy. "Done?"

"Not yet."

I fidgeted. "Are you *sure* it's not too short?"

"Positive." Marie applied a layer of lip gloss, grabbed a piece of toilet paper, and said, "Blot." I pressed my lips down on the toilet paper. "There. Now you're ready to go."

I peeked in the mirror. Smoky gray eyes and black eyeliner stared back at me, making my eyes seem brighter than usual. And the red lip gloss actually looked…good. "Wow."

"Right?" Marie put the rest of the makeup away, fluffed her blonde hair, and grinned. "We'll be the prettiest girls there. Now let's go."

We linked arms and walked out of the dorm. As we passed, boys gaped at us, making me smile. Okay, maybe Marie was right. Maybe I needed this. After Finn kissed me and practically wiped his mouth to remove my taste from his lips, my self-esteem had been lagging. It might be fun to go out and drink. Flirt a little bit too much.

And then Finn could kiss my un-kissable ass.

Marie dropped my arm when we reached the crowded frat house. Girls in dresses even shorter than mine filled the room, as well as guys in plaid shorts and solid-colored shirts. From a distance, they all looked the same. Marie tugged me toward the "bar" area, which was really just a bunch of wine coolers and beer cans on a folding table. "Which one do you want?"

I eyed the choices skeptically, then reached for a pink drink with a picture of the beach on the label. "This one, I guess."

"Good choice." Marie opened it for me and grabbed a beer from the table. After opening her own drink, she nodded to the room. "Next assignment is for you to find a cute guy and start talking to him. Think of this like a class. A class at how to party properly."

I rolled my eyes. "But—"

I turned around and Marie was gone, already chatting up a guy I vaguely recognized. Great. Just freaking great. Now what? Everywhere I looked, people were already engrossed in conversations. I wasn't the type of girl who just barged in and invaded other people's conversations. Giving up on finding someone who wasn't already busy, I scanned the room, looking for somewhere to sit. As I searched, I tilted my drink to my lips. It tasted sweet and a little bit like pink lemonade.

Whoever came up with this type of alcohol was *brilliant*.

Spying an empty spot by the door, I carefully made my way across the room in my heels and sat down on the step leading outside. I hadn't left, but it gave me room to breathe. It was a win-win. No sooner had I sat down than a man was next to me, a beer in his hand and a sloppy grin on his face.

"Hey, there," he said, his voice slurred. "Haven't seen you around here before."

How many drinks had he had? I got nervous around drunk people. They were too unpredictable. Dad had thrown a dinner party once and a man had gotten drunk and punched another guy for looking at his wife too long. He'd been perfectly fine, and even polite, before the drinking.

Though my urge to run was strong, I forced myself to take a sip of my drink. I'd been running away enough. It was time to stand still. "Yeah, I'm new here."

"Freshman?"

"Yep." I took another sip. The drink was delicious. "You?"

He scooted closer to me, pressing his body against mine. I could smell the alcohol on his breath, overwhelming and sickening. "I'm a junior."

I stiffened. Though Finn had done the same thing earlier, his body pressed to mine hadn't made me want to gag. It hadn't made me feel like a thousand worms squiggled under my skin. I scooted away from him. "Nice."

He reached out and played with my hair, leaning so close that his beer breath washed over me. "I like this color. Is it real?"

"Uh, yeah." I pulled my hair free and slid into the corner of the banister. "What's your major?"

"You are," he said, following me.

That had to be the corniest line I had ever heard or read. And I'd read a heck of a lot of books. I couldn't help it. I laughed. "Okay, that was funny."

"It's only the beginning."

Without warning, his lips closed over mine. Instead of the electric whir I had felt when Finn kissed me, the itchy need to get closer to him…I couldn't breathe. I tore free of this man's smothering mouth, but he moved on to my neck without a second's hesitation.

"Get off me." Shoving at his shoulders, I stood up and took a calming breath. After setting my half empty bottle on the step, I said, "I have a boyfriend."

"Oh. Why didn't you tell me before you kissed me?" Beer Breath asked. He stumbled to his feet and adjusted his junk.

So freaking attractive.

"I didn't—"

"Get lost," a hard voice that I recognized said from the shadows. "You'll go back to your stupid little party and find another drunk girl to hit on."

"Says who?" Beer Breath asked, a cocky grin on his face.

"Says me," Finn said, stepping out of the shadows. He flexed his fists and stepped closer to me. "Go ahead. Give me a reason to punch your fucking face in, and I'll gladly oblige."

Beer Breath paled and shuffled backward. "Dude. She kissed me."

"No, I didn't."

"We wouldn't expect you to know the difference, now would we?" Finn asked, his voice mocking. He was practically begging for a fight. And all because of what? Because some dude kissed me? Why did he even care? "You have five seconds to be gone."

Beer Breath turned red. "You know what? Run off with your little boyfriend and don't ever come back to this frat again."

Beer Breath stormed off, leaving Finn and me alone on the porch. I pivoted and gave him what I hoped was an annoyed look. "You do realize I can handle a grabby-hands boy by myself, right? I dealt with you, after all."

He stepped closer, towering over me. "Ginger, you have no idea how to deal with me."

I stiffened. "I know that if I kissed you now, you wouldn't push me away."

"Of course I wouldn't. Look at you." His gaze dipped over my body, and when he met my eyes again his own were blazing and hot. "Any man would kiss you back."

"You'd push me away after."

He lifted a shoulder but said nothing.

He was so darn condescending and cocky. "Why are you at another frat party that I just *happen* to be at? Who are you? Why are you following me?"

Finn leaned against a palm tree and looked far too casual, but he reminded me of one of those lions on the Discovery Channel. He looked perfectly calm on the surface, but in a second he could be all deadly and lethal. "I'm here because I was taking a walk down the beach, and I saw you and that loser kissing. Then I saw you push him away. I wanted to make sure you were okay, but now I'm wishing I had bashed his head into the fucking wall before I let him go."

My heart rose to my throat. "Why?"

"Because you should be kissing *me*," he practically whispered. "Not some college boy who doesn't know what he's doing."

He closed the distance between us. And as soon as his hands were on my hips, his mouth was on mine. The familiar sensations he'd awoken in me came to life, and I clung to him. His tongue entwined with mine, and he grabbed my waist, yanking me against him.

I lifted up on tiptoe, trying to get closer, and moaned softly. He needed to do that again. And more. This is how a kiss was supposed to feel. This is what it was supposed to do to me. I might be inexperienced, but even I knew what a good kiss felt like.

And. This. Was. It.

CHAPTER SIX

Finn

As soon as my lips touched hers, I knew I was making one of the biggest fucking mistakes of my life. I shouldn't have done that. I *really* shouldn't have done that. Seeing her in that bastard's arms had triggered something deep within me. Something had made me go crazy and come down on her like a barbarian or some shit like that. I'd needed to show her who she should really be kissing. That same primal urge had apparently taken away the common sense God had given me. This was strictly off limits. Forbidden.

Yet I couldn't stop.

When she whimpered into my mouth and pressed even closer to me, pressing her soft stomach against my hard cock, I wanted so badly to forget all the reasons why I couldn't kiss her. Forget all the reasons I couldn't bring her back to my place and spend all night making her scream my name.

But then my phone buzzed.

And all the reasons I *shouldn't* be kissing her came flooding back. I jerked free and stumbled back, a hand over my mouth. As if that would help remove the memory of how wonderful she tasted. "Fuck."

She stiffened, her sapphire eyes going narrow. "No. Fuck *you*." Flinging her hair over her shoulder, she headed for the dorms.

I ignored my phone and stumbled after her. "Wait. I'm sorry."

"Sorry about what?" She spun around, arms akimbo and eyes blazing. "Sorry you kissed me again? Sorry you keep kissing me and then regretting it? Sorry you keep following me around?" She shoved my shoulders hard, but I didn't move. Not much could move me anymore. "What's your deal, anyway?"

I clenched my jaw. "The truth is, I don't want to want you. I'm a Marine. I could be out of this place in days for all I know. And I barely know you, and yet I can't stay away. That's what I'm doing here. That's why I keep coming back."

Even if it is my job to follow you around.

"Why aren't you supposed to want me?" Her eyes went wide and she pointed a finger at me. "Oh my God, you have a girlfriend. Don't you?"

My heart stuttered to a stop before speeding up painfully. For a second, I thought she knew who I really was. For a second, I thought my cover had been blown. And I had been relieved. Maybe I needed to stop this game. Quit.

"No. I don't." I held my hands out to my sides, palms up. "I'm not a cheater."

"Just a player."

No, just a liar. "Pretty much. And I'm already committed to my work."

She pressed her lips together. "The Marines."

I wanted to correct her. Tell her it was my other job that was causing problems, but then she'd want more info. Info I couldn't give her. "Right."

She smoothed her hair. "So what are we supposed to do? Stop seeing each other?"

I couldn't do that even if my job *wasn't* to see her. I wanted to be with her, plain and simple; no matter how wrong it might be. "No. I can't do that."

"Then what do you want from me?" She tilted her head back and looked up at me, her lips soft and her eyes even softer. I wanted to kiss her again, but I held back. "You aren't making any sense."

"I want to…I want to teach you to surf, and ride on my bike, and be with you, but I can't *be with* you."

I cupped her cheek and kissed her forehead. Her lids drifted shut, and she swayed closer. It took all my control to not capture her lips. To not take what she so freely offered, but she didn't realize who she offered her lips to. If she knew she would hate me.

More than I hated myself right now.

She held on to my biceps and gave me a small smile. "Friends?"

"Friends."

She nodded and dropped her hold on me. I let her go, but it was hard. Way too fucking hard. "Then you can't be mad if you see me kissing other guys. You can't not want me, but not want me to be with someone else. That's not fair."

The hell it wasn't.

"I can't promise that." I gritted my teeth. "I don't make promises I can't keep, and I don't think I can keep that one."

"Then at least promise you won't lie to me anymore." She canted her head. "Can you promise me that?"

I swallowed hard. "I can't promise that either," I managed to say. "But I can promise to do my best not to hurt you and to be a good friend."

She gave me one last look and turned on her heel, leaving me behind. I followed her, even though I had been clearly dismissed. Yep. She was just like her father. "Would you rather I lie and say I'll never tell you a lie? Who can promise that?"

"Honest people. That's who."

I laughed hard. "So you've never lied to me?"

She hesitated. I could see her recalling our time together, going over every conversation in detail. After licking her lips, she finally admitted, "No. I guess I can't say that."

"See?" Of course, I already knew all about the lies she'd told me. Every single one. "No one can promise that. People lie all the time, especially when it comes to little things."

My phone buzzed again, but I ignored it. Hers buzzed too and she pulled it out. After quickly typing on her phone, she gave me her attention again. "Fine. You win." Her phone buzzed again and she rolled her eyes. "What is he even doing up?"

"Who?" I asked, even though I knew who it was. I hadn't answered his text soon enough, so he'd texted his daughter. The dude needed some form of medication and some *serious* help.

"My dad." She stole a quick peek at me as she texted. "He's kind of crazy protective."

"No kidding."

She snorted. "I wish I was kidding. It's, like, after midnight there."

"Where are you from?"

She froze, her fingers hovering over her iPhone screen. "Washington, D.C."

"Nice." I rocked back on my heels, slipping back into my role. It was time to play the part of interested friend again. Asking questions I already knew the answer to. "What does he do?"

"Oh, nothing too interesting." She put her phone away and gave me a calculating stare. "Something to do with billing."

Or *making* bills. "Oh, that sounds fun."

"Not really," she said, smiling. "It's pretty boring. What do your parents do?"

"My mom died of cancer when I was sixteen." I ignored the pang of pain I still felt at the loss. There was no use living in the past, and it would never go away. "My dad is in security."

She placed a hand on my shoulder. "I'm so sorry for you loss. I can't even imagine…"

I knew she was close with her mother. Much closer than she was to her father, who seemed determined to run her life for her, no matter how old she might be. "Thanks."

"Can friends hug?"

"Hell yeah they can."

She flung her arms around my neck, holding me close. For a second, my arms lingered at her hips, but then I let myself pull her close. I may have buried my face in her neck, but that was pure speculation I would deny even under torture if asked later.

She stepped back and grinned up at me. "So…surfing tomorrow?"

"Sure." I headed toward her dorm room, but she didn't follow me. I stopped walking. "Hello?'

She grinned. "Hi."

"Why aren't you coming with me?"

"I have to go back to the party." She pointed over her shoulder. "Marie's waiting for me. I promised her I wouldn't leave early again."

I stiffened. I didn't like the thought of her hanging out with more guys like the one who'd just kissed her. "You're going back to that place? To that guy?"

"Yeah, I can handle him."

She started for the party, but I grabbed her elbow. "Don't go. Those places are asking for trouble. What if something bad happens?"

She raised her brows. "What if it doesn't?"

"At least let me go with you."

"Nope." She wiggled free and started walking again. "I want to be on my own. I'm ready to go back into the masses. If I'm going to be in college, I have to get used to this type of thing, right?"

"You don't have to party to be in college," I said tightly. "You can, ya know, study."

"I plan on doing that." She stopped on the steps of the party. The loud music came out the windows, and I could see a couple getting pretty hot and heavy almost directly behind her. Would that be her soon? "But tonight I'm being someone besides myself. And I'm going to go have some fun, even if it kills me."

It might not kill her, but she might be the death of me.

She wiggled her fingers in my direction and disappeared inside the building. I stood there awkwardly, my hands in my pockets, and shifted on my feet so I could see her. She grabbed another wine cooler and made her way over to a young man sitting in the corner. He had blond hair and screamed of money.

He was probably born with a silver spoon in his mouth, just like Carrie. He wore high-quality clothing and his Rolex glinted in the dim lighting. The boy looked up at her as if she were a goddess and moved over so she could sit beside him. They conversed quietly, and then the boy laughed at something Carrie said.

While I watched from outside, like someone who didn't belong.

Because I didn't, in more ways than one.

CHAPTER SEVEN

Carrie

The next morning, I struggled to get to the surface, my lungs bursting with the need to breathe. The need for air. I kicked wildly but seemed to be getting nowhere fast. I knew time was running out. Knew I needed to breathe sooner rather than later. If I died in this ocean, Dad would kill me.

Finn had given me a ten-minute lecture about the dangers of surfing. Telling me to never leave his side, never take a wave that wasn't the right size for me, never take chances, and above all—never disobey him out in the ocean. Out there, he was my boss and I would "fucking listen." Well, I had followed all those rules. I had fucking listened.

But I was *still* drowning.

Just as I was certain I would never see the light of day again, a strong hand closed around my wrist and tugged me to the surface. As I gulped in a deep breath, the air stinging my oxygen-deprived lungs, I opened my eyes and saw Finn looking down at me with a tight jaw. Little droplets of water spiked on his long lashes, and his hair was soaking wet.

"Got you," he said, his voice rough.

"Thanks," I sputtered, struggling to catch my breath. I shivered, and he frowned down at me even more. "It's c-cold under there."

"Yeah. I noticed," he said. A muscle ticked in his jaw again. What was his deal? "You almost drowned. You know that, right?"

"I was fine." And I was also a big fat liar. I hadn't been fine. Far from it. And truth be told? I'd been terrified. But that was all the more reason for me to keep going. To try again until I got better. I refused to back down. "Ready to go again?"

"Hell no. You're done for today, no matter what you say," he said, paddling toward the shore and towing me behind him like an errant child. "If I have to save your life one more time today, you'll owe me your first born son."

I could fight his hold and insist on continuing, but the truth was I was worn out. I could feel my exhaustion all the way to my bones. We'd been in the water for three hours. I was tired, achy, and freezing. California water might look inviting, but it was freaking frigid. "F-Fine. We'll do it again next weekend."

He shot me an incredulous look. "You want to go back out?"

"Of course," I said through numb lips. "I want to learn."

"You're something else," he muttered, shaking his head.

"W-What's that supposed to mean?"

He lifted a shoulder. "I would've thought one time would be enough for you."

"I don't give up easily." As soon as my feet hit sand, I pulled free of his grip. His assumptions about me were getting awfully annoying. "I get my steely determination from my father and my need to succeed from my mother. So don't *assume* I'll quit so easily."

"Relax. I didn't mean to insult you."

"You did."

I waited for him to apologize. To say he was wrong about me. Good thing I didn't hold my breath, because I'd have died waiting. Instead, he shot me an amused look and slung his board under his arm. When he reached for mine, I shook my head and mimicked his hold with my own.

"Refusing help now?" he asked, his eyes lighting up with amusement.

I had to know how to do this myself. He wouldn't always be with me. "I don't need you doting all over me, thank you very much."

"Doting?" he spluttered, his face turning red. "I'm not *doting* on you. Christ."

"I'm perfectly capable of carrying my own board."

"Unbelievable," he muttered under his breath. He shook his head and walked toward our towels. "Take off the wetsuit."

46

I looked down at the only thing keeping me warm right now. "Why? That doesn't make any sense."

"Can you *not* argue for one time in your life?"

"Excuse me for speaking my mind, master." I stiffened. "I'd say it'll never happen again, but it would be a lie."

He laughed. "Just trust me, okay? You'll warm up quicker without the suit." He held out my towel. "And put this on once you're out of it."

Why did I have to wear a towel? Maybe he couldn't stand the sight of me. "Right here?"

He cocked a brow. "Yeah. What's wrong? You naked under there?"

"No, of course not." I looked around. A bunch of surfers were stripping out of their suits without a shred of modesty a few feet over, chatting about the waves that would be coming from the storm tonight. Apparently undressing in public was normal. "I just didn't realize…"

I drifted off, feeling stupid. It's not like my bikini I wore underneath was something I never showed anyone. It was meant to be worn out in public, for Pete's sake. I might be undressing in public in front of a bunch of men, but it was a bikini. No big deal.

After taking a deep breath to calm my stupidly racing heart, I peeled the wetsuit off my body. For a brief second, I thought my bikini top had gone off with the suit, but a quick glance showed it was still in place—but slightly skewed. As I adjusted the top, I lifted my head and found Finn watching me with dark eyes. As our gazes collided, he turned away.

I had caught him watching me, and the look in his eyes had sent a fist of something crashing through me. Desire? Need? Both.

God, he didn't make any sense. He watched me as if he couldn't get his mind off me, and yet he kept insisting he couldn't have me. Heaven forbid another man looked my way though. He'd be all over the guy in two seconds flat, just like a jealous boyfriend. All the cons without the pros.

I tugged the wetsuit past my hips, but stopped when I realized the wetsuit wasn't the only thing I was removing. "Oops. My bikini bottom almost came off."

"Please make sure it doesn't," he said over his shoulder. "Unless you want to put on a show for a bunch of older men."

Were they all older? I scanned the men surrounding us. A guy was about my age leaned against a tree, his eyes on me. "They're not all old.

The guy watching me over there is my age. Actually, he's kind of cute..."

Finn spun around so fast he should have gotten whiplash. Within seconds, he was in front of me, his hands on my hips and his back pressed to my front. "Who? Where?"

Yep. Jealous boyfriend, only without the perks. No way I was letting him go all alpha male on the poor guy for daring to look at me. "I think he might have left."

I pretended to look around his wide shoulders, leaning against his back for support. When my breasts brushed against his damp skin, my already hard nipples pebbled into even harder beads, seeming to beg for his touch. Could he tell? Did he know? When he tensed up and drew in a deep breath, I got my answer. "Fuck, Carrie. What are you doing?"

"Just looking around for that guy," I breathed, finding boldness in his obvious reaction to me. "Why? Is something wrong?"

"You aren't ready for what you're starting, Ginger."

Yeah, I was. *He* was the one who wasn't ready. Not me.

I didn't know what struck me, what made me think that I could seduce him. I didn't know what the hell I was doing. He'd probably been with countless women, while I was nothing but a nineteen-year-old virgin who read too many romance books. One who didn't know what to do with a man like Finn.

But I tried anyway. I trailed my fingers over his shoulders, then leaned in and pressed a kiss to the back of his shoulder. Reaching around him, I let my hands slide down his hard pecs, toward his abs. He tensed and hissed through his teeth. I bit down on his shoulder and tried to get up the nerve to go even lower.

He shuddered and leaned back into me, his hands reaching around to grab my butt. His fingers fanned out over the top of my thighs, so close to touching me where I needed him most, yet not close enough. "Carrie..." he said, his voice strained. "You need to...I need to...back away. Now. Or you'll be mine in more ways than you can handle. Right here. Right now. In front of everyone."

After a second of hesitation, I backed off, the intensity in his voice almost too much for me to handle. I didn't doubt that he meant it. That he would kiss me in front of everyone. But surely not...not what he said. He acted as if he was about to bend me over the bench and have his way with me.

"You wouldn't." I pressed my hands to my cheeks, which suddenly felt way too hot.

"I would." He spun to face me, his face red. "What game are you playing?"

My gaze fell to his erection, which strained against his swim trunks. He wanted me, just like I wanted him. I swallowed past the Sahara Desert that was now my throat and forced my eyes northward. "I'm not playing any games. I just wanted—"

"I know what you wanted." He flexed his jaw and stepped back from me. His gaze dipped below my face for a second, but then he turned around again. My stomach coiled, as if he'd touched me instead of simply looking my way. "Put the towel on."

I scowled at his back. If he wanted to ignore the desire between us, I would let him, but I didn't have to make it *easy* on him. After drying my hair, I flung the towel across the bench before I sat down and reclined against the seat. Covering a yawn with my hand, I dropped my head back against the wood.

"You got something against a towel?" he asked.

"Yeah. I want to feel the sun."

"Feel it through a towel," he said.

"Nah. I'm good." I bit my lower lip to keep it from lifting into a smile. I kind of liked the fact that he couldn't bear seeing me. At least, now that I knew *why*. "That was fun but exhausting."

I heard him move closer, but didn't open my eyes. "Maybe you're tired because of the partying and not the surfing," he said.

"I doubt it." I cracked one eye open to look at him. He was watching me, but he wasn't staring at my face. "Though, I did meet a nice guy."

His fists went even tighter. "Oh yeah?"

"Yeah. His name's Cory." I shrugged. "He gave me his number. We're in a bunch of classes together, and we even have the same major."

He was exactly the kind of man Dad would pick for me. The kind of guy he would want to call his son-in-law. If they ever met, Dad would probably start drawing up wedding invitations within minutes of meeting Cory. I, however, preferred my men with tattoos and attitude and perpetually disheveled hair.

Men like Finn.

"How perfect," he said, his voice tight. "I'm sure Daddy would approve of him."

My eyes flew open. His thoughts mirrored my own way too well. "Excuse me?"

"I-I mean, he sounds like the kind of guy a father would like." He sat down beside me, hanging his hands in between his knees. "From what little I know of fathers, anyway."

I relaxed again. For a second, I thought he knew something more about me than he should have. "Did any of your girlfriends' fathers like you?"

He shrugged. "I haven't really had any. I've been married to my work for the past five years. Not much free time."

"Oh." I looked at him out of the corner of my eye. "I can't imagine you being single. I figured a guy like you would have numerous women in his life."

"Now who's making assumptions?" he asked, giving me a pointed look.

"I'm sorry," I quickly said. I hated when he did it to me, and I'd gone and done it to him. "I didn't mean to be rude."

"Apology accepted, but it just so happens you might be right."

My jaw dropped open. He didn't make any sense. "You said you've been single."

"I've been single." He grinned at me. "Not celibate. Two different things."

I rolled my eyes, disappointed by his honesty. I'd been hoping... what, exactly? That he'd spent his whole life waiting for the right girl to come along? As if.

He shifted on the bench and stole a glance at me. "Are you going to see this guy again?"

"I'm sure I will. We do have classes together."

He sighed. "I meant outside of school."

"I don't know." I looked up, watching the clouds move lazily across the blue sky. One of the clouds looked like the Washington Monument, and it made me miss home and my mom. Heck, even my dad.

"What's his last name?"

I eyed him. "Why?"

"Just curious if I knew him."

"Oh. Pinkerton." I watched the monument cloud until in merged with another, making it unrecognizable. "I'll probably see him again. He seems nice."

"Nice," he muttered. "That's a word for a puppy, not a man. Nice won't make you scream out in bed."

I choked on a laugh, but something inside of me responded differently. Finn would probably be able to make me scream his name. Too bad he didn't want to. "I can't believe you said that."

He lifted a shoulder. "If the shoe fits…"

"Well, I like puppies and nice guys like Cory," I added. Even though I was lying. I much preferred Finn.

"You're a dog person?" he asked.

"Some dogs." I smiled and pictured Mom's dog running through the yard with a pink bow around its neck. "I like the little terrier my mom has. She's cute."

"Do you miss home?"

"Yeah." I nodded and swallowed hard. "I mean, it's been less than a week, but I definitely miss certain things. Although it's nice being on my own. Making friends. Surfing. Riding a motorcycle." I hesitated. I wanted to tell him more about myself. Wanted to trust him. "I couldn't do that stuff at home. There were too many eyes on me all the time."

"Too many eyes," he said softly. "That doesn't sound fun."

"It kind of sucked," I admitted. "My dad is kind of…important in his company. He's in politics, and with politics…people are always watching."

He cleared his throat. "You didn't mention that before."

"I didn't trust you before." I met his eyes and bit down on my lip. "I do now. I'm hoping it's not a mistake."

"It's not," he said, but his eyes looked shaded with something I couldn't name. "I won't tell anyone."

"Yeah, I'm trying to keep a low profile. I look a lot different than I used to, and I was lucky enough to be out of the media for the last year. Hopefully it stays that way."

"So, you're like a Kennedy?"

I laughed. I wasn't nearly so high up on the political food chain, nor did I want to be. "Hardly so glamorous."

He elbowed me in the ribs. "I like the idea of being friends with a Kennedy. It sounds impressive, don't ya think?"

"No," I managed to say with a straight face, but then I ruined it by laughing. "I'm not as cool as them."

"I think you're just fine the way you are," he said. "How did you manage to come here without security?"

My breath caught in my throat, but I refused to read into that too much. "Dad wanted to send private security with me, but I refused. He probably sent some out here anyway, knowing him."

He tugged on his hair. "Do you think he'd do that?"

"I *know* he'd do that." I played with the string on the side of my bikini bottoms, not wanting to look at him when I told him this part. "They're probably watching us right now."

He gave an uneasy laugh. "If so, they'll probably kick my ass for taking you surfing."

"If they're smart, they'll never show their faces."

He snorted. "Should they be scared of you?"

"Scared of how I'll react? Yes." I stood up and held out my hands. "I want to be normal. Have normal fun and kiss normal boys. Study late at night and party occasionally. Is that so *wrong*?"

"Whoa." He stood up and grabbed my hands. "I didn't say it was."

"I know. Sorry." The righteous anger seemed to disappear, leaving me as deflated as a leaky balloon. "I get all worked up when I think of those sickos out there, following me around. Watching everything I do. I mean, get a life. Who in their right mind takes a job watching someone else 24/7? It's like being a glorified stalker if you ask me."

He gave an uneasy laugh. "Come on. Let's get some coffee and forget all about the men possibly watching us."

"All right." I took a deep breath and dropped one of his hands. "This time, it's on me."

He stiffened. "I'd rather—"

"And so would I. We're not dating. We're friends, and friends split bills."

He hesitated. "They do," he admitted. "I have to ask. Why is it you never had friends?"

"Uh…" I nibbled on my lower lip. "Well, not many of them passed by Dad's scrutiny. If their parents had even a whiff of scandal attached to their names, we were done hanging out. The few who did pass were major bitches."

"Ah." His fingers flexed on mine. "What about boyfriends?"

"Please," I scoffed. "Do you really think they passed Daddy's test?"

He flinched. "That bad, huh?"

"Worse. I stopped trying after tenth grade."

"What about in Europe?"

"Not a chance." I tightened my grip on his hand. "I had security with me the whole time. I met a cute Italian boy while I was there, but that was it."

His thumb stroked the back of my hand. "*Ciao, bella.*"

"You speak Italian?"

"Nope. That's all I know," he admitted, laughing. Dropping my hand, he stopped at the coffee stand and propelled me forward with a hand splayed across my lower back. "Ladies first."

My cheeks went all hot, and my body all tingly. From a simple touch. "Uh, a nonfat iced mocha, please."

"I'll have a black coffee," he said, smiling at the barista.

The barista almost dropped the cup in her hand, then dipped her head low. I rolled my eyes, but realized I probably looked that stupid around him half of the time. I shook my head. "Don't you ever branch out? Try something new?"

He eyed me from under his shades. "I like my coffee black."

"Did you ever get a mocha or a latte?"

"Nope." He shuddered. "I don't drink girly coffee."

"It's not girly. Besides, if you've never had it, then you can't know that you don't like it." I headed for the end of the counter. His hand stayed on my back, as if he didn't want to let me go. And I didn't want him to let me go. I pulled a twenty out of my bikini top and handed it to the cashier. It had actually stayed dry.

"Because I know." He cleared his throat. "Did you seriously just take money out of your bra to pay?"

"It's not a bra. It's a bikini." I shot him a grin over my shoulder. "But yeah. Strippers do it, why not surfers?"

He grabbed my coffee and handed it to me. "Did you know two out of six dollar bills have been shoved down a stripper's G-string at one point in time?"

"No." I shuddered. "Thanks for that."

I dropped all the ones I'd gotten back into the tip jar and walked toward our bench. Our surfboards still sat there. God, I loved California. In D.C., they would have been gone within seconds. I could get used to this place. Used to the way of life. Especially the cute surfer boys who came with it.

"So, you ready for school to start tomorrow?" he asked, blowing on his coffee as he sat down beside me.

"Yeah, I guess so." I held out my drink and pressed my straw to his lips. "Take a sip."

He clamped his mouth shut and shook his head. "No."

"For me?"

His eyes flashed. "You don't play fair."

"I'm the daughter of a politician. What did you expect?"

"Touché." He leaned in, closed his lips around the straw, and took a sip. When he pulled back, he swallowed. "It's not too bad, I guess, but I'll stick with my black coffee."

"Hm." I lifted the cup to my own lips and sipped. I couldn't help but think that my lips were where his had just been. I wished he would kiss me again. Wished he would stop being all honorable and stuff. As I pulled back, I flicked my tongue over the tip of the straw. "Tastes good to me."

He leaned in, his gaze on my mouth. I held my breath, waiting to see what he would do. Waiting to see if he'd stop fighting and start kissing, but he froze a few breaths away from me. "It's okay." He leaned back against the bench and took a long swig of his coffee. "So, what else are you doing today, Ginger?"

Hello, change of topic. "I have this thing," I mumbled.

He sat forward. "What thing?"

"Does it matter?"

His gaze pinned me down. Made it hard to concentrate. "Yes. Friends tell each other their plans."

"What are yours?"

"I'm going to lay around in my boxers and watch TV all night. Maybe drink a few beers." He pointed at me with his coffee. "Your turn."

I was too busy picturing him in his boxers to fight him. "I'm going to the soup kitchen to help serve Sunday dinner."

He paused with his cup halfway to his lips. "Seriously?"

"Seriously." I took a long sip of coffee, uncomfortable with his

54

scrutiny. "It's important to give back to the community."

He set his coffee down and cupped my chin with his thumb and finger. "You're one amazing woman. You know that, right, Ginger?"

The nickname that had once annoyed me sent shivers through my veins now. "Not really. I'm just a college girl."

"Most college students are too busy partying to care about feeding the poor."

"I've gotta share what I can." I shrugged. "It's only right. Karma and all that."

He pressed his lips together, seeming to be stopping himself from saying something. "I'm going with you. I want to help."

"You don't have to," I protested, even though my whole body quickened at the thought of spending more time with him. "I'll be fine on my own."

"I know you will." He brushed his thumb over my lip. "But I *want* to go with you."

"All right," I said breathlessly. "Wanna pick me up on the bike at six?"

He laughed. "I created a beast with that thing, didn't I?"

"Yep." I stood up, tossed out my empty coffee and grabbed my surfboard. "I'll be waiting. Don't be late."

CHAPTER EIGHT

Carrie

It was almost time to meet up with Finn, so I hurried down the stairs, my heart beating a little bit faster than usual. After I warned him not to be late, there was no way I could be late myself. He'd never let that slide. As I passed the last dorm in my hallway, a girl came out and grabbed my wrist. "Hey, you the one who put all those designer clothes in the communal room?"

"Uh, no." Well, crap. I didn't think anyone had seen me earlier. I tucked my hair behind my ear and smiled. "I have no idea what you're talking about."

The girl adjusted her top. The top I had put in a box for others to take a few hours ago. "Darn. I could've sworn they said it was the redhead in 123."

Well, there went my career as a super spy. I had tried to be sneaky about it, but I couldn't help but share some of the clothes my mom constantly sent me with the other people in my dorm. I mean, why not? I'd seen and heard how some of the students didn't have much money for clothes…and I had too many. That's all. "Nope. Wrong room."

"Oh, well, sorry. I just wanted to say thanks. I've always wanted a Gucci top."

I smiled and waved over my shoulder as I started down the hallway. "Well, if I figure out who it is, I'll pass the message along."

"Thanks."

I made a mental note to put more Gucci out next time Mom sent a care package. Most of the stuff went to the local homeless shelters, but it didn't hurt to anonymously help my fellow classmates, did it? As I pushed through the doors to the outside, I smiled at the sight of Finn waiting for me. He leaned against a tree, looking completely at ease in his board shorts and red T-shirt. His ink stood out even more against the contrast of the red. When I approached him, he cocked a brow.

"*I'm* on time."

"So am I. Look at us, being all grown up and stuff." I patted his arm. Hot damn, his arm was hard. And huge. "You ready?"

"Yeah."

He fell into step beside me, like he always did. I wished I was bold enough to grab his hand again, but he'd clearly told me he didn't want anything to do with me, romance-wise. So I kept my grabby hands to myself. "Have you ever helped out at a shelter before?"

"No." He stole a quick look at me. "That's probably pretty crappy of me, huh?"

I shook my head. "Nah."

"Why do you do it?"

"Why not?" I stopped at his motorcycle. As I watched, he climbed on and handed me his helmet. Maybe I should have went out and bought my own earlier. Then he would stop insisting I use his. Would that look too forward? Be too pushy? I had no idea. "Shouldn't you be wearing this instead of me?"

"No." He looked over his shoulder at me. "Now put it on."

I took the helmet. I could argue, but I knew when it came to my safety, he wouldn't budge. He was a lot like Dad in that respect. Once again, the niggling doubt that said he'd been sent here by my father to befriend me came to mind. I shoved it down as best I could. Finn hadn't given me any reason to suspect him. Just because the past hadn't worked out so well for me didn't mean history was repeating itself.

After shoving the helmet over my head, I climbed on behind him and held on tight. The whole ride to the soup kitchen, I went over all the different ways he'd proved he wasn't Dad's lackey. He'd kissed me—which Dad would never allow. Taken me surfing—which Dad would hate. Driven me around on his bike—which Dad would flip his shit over. And he was…Finn.

There was no way Dad would send a guy who looked like Finn to protect me unless he was blind, dumb, and stupid. Or incredibly naïve.

We turned into the parking lot, and he shut off the bike. I removed the helmet and handed it to him, but he was too busy scanning our surroundings as if the Big Bad Wolf lurked in the shadows or something. I nudged him with the helmet and he took it without taking his eyes off the people around us. "I don't like this setting."

I followed his gaze, but saw nothing out of place. A man in tattered clothing sat on the ground outside the door, but he looked harmless. Hungry, but harmless. A woman leaned against the wall a few feet past him, watching us. Her face was filthy, but her eyes seemed kind. "Don't be a hypocrite. These people just need food."

Finn looked at me again. His face softened and he cupped my cheek. I liked it when he did that, but I had to remember it meant nothing to him. Not like it did to me. "Your kindness might be the death of you."

I climbed off his bike, letting his hand fall to his lap. He quickly followed me, staying close by my side. I stopped walking, giving him a stern look. "I don't need protecting."

"I'm not." He threw an arm over my shoulders. "I'm just being friendly."

I rolled my eyes. "Yeah. Sure." As I approached the woman I'd seen earlier, I reached into my pocket, took out a gift card to McDonald's, and pressed it into the woman's hand. "Here. For this week."

The woman took the card and smiled at me, her eyes lighting up. "Thank you."

I nodded, uncomfortable with the gratitude. This should be something more people did, and it shouldn't bring about such appreciation. I wished I could help everyone. I went to the man on the other side of the door and did the same. He thanked me and fell back asleep.

As we entered the building, Finn shook his head. "Does your father know you do this?"

"No." I tucked my hair behind my ear. "I use the money he sends me every month. He always sends twice what I need. Sometimes more."

Finn fell silent, but he looked at me weird. As if I was an enigma he couldn't figure out, which was silly. It was a simple matter. I had money, they didn't. Easily fixed. It wasn't exactly rocket science.

We walked up to the woman who looked to be in charge. "Hi. I'm Carrie, and this is Finn. We're here to help."

The woman eyed me. Her weathered face cracked into a disapproving frown. I'd been judged and found wanting within seconds. "You okay with getting your hands dirty? A pretty little thing like you?"

Finn stiffened. "Excuse me? I'll have you know—"

"It's okay." I placed a hand on his arm. There he went again, going into knight-in-shining-armor mode. It was cute and all, but I could take care of myself. "I'll be fine. Where do you want us?"

"The kitchens. You're on dish duty."

I nodded and headed for the kitchen. Finn started to follow me, but the woman stopped him by stepping in his path. She barely reached the bottom of Finn's shoulders, but he stopped instantly. "Not you. You're out front. Watch for trouble and break it up if it starts."

He hesitated. "I'm with her."

"I'll be fine back there." I shooed him away. "Go be a protective Marine for someone else tonight."

"All right." He gave me a hard look. "Don't leave this building without me. Not even for air."

I saluted him. "Yes, sir."

He grinned. "Good girl."

I shook my head and headed into the kitchen. The whole way there, I could feel his eyes on me, but once I got inside the kitchen, I was too busy to focus on Finn. The rest of my night was spent scrubbing filthy dishes. By the time I was finished, I was coated in a sheen of sweat and feeling pretty darn gross.

I came out of the kitchen and scanned the room for Finn. He was at the door, his arms crossed. He looked more like a bouncer at a popular nightclub than a volunteer. I shook my head and smiled. He looked as out of place here as I did at the fancy balls Mom always dragged me to.

The woman in charge came up to me. "Thank you for the help."

"Thanks for letting us contribute." I swiped my wrist across my sticky forehead and then reached into my pocket. "Do you mind if I leave these with you? If any families come in, or anyone you know who needs the extra help, just give them one."

The woman took the gift cards, but her forehead wrinkled. "Are these all from you?"

"They're from Senator Wallington. He likes supporting the less fortunate."

The woman's eyes lit up. "Wow. A politician who actually cares?"

"He tries." If Dad ever found out about me spending the funds he sent me on someone else, I could at least point out that it helped his campaign. That would end the lecture pretty fast. I squeezed the woman's shoulder and winked. "Remember him if he's ever up for president."

"I will," the woman said, wonder in her voice. She headed straight for a family eating in the corner and gave them two cards. When the family looked my way, I smiled and headed for the door. Time for me to leave.

Finn stood there, watching me. When I reached his side, he looked at the family who had just received the gift cards. "More Robin Hood acts?"

"Yeah. And?"

"Nothing." He shook his head. "Let's go home and eat something ourselves. I'm starving."

My stomach chose that particular moment to sound like a hungry beast. I pressed a hand to it and smiled at him. "Deal."

"Islands?"

"What?"

"Don't tell me you've never been to Islands…"

"I've never even heard of it. What is it?"

"Only the best burgers this side of the Mississippi." He handed me his helmet. "I solemnly swear that you'll never be able to eat McDonald's again once you've tasted their burgers."

I laughed. God, he made everything so much fun. "Oh yeah?" I put the helmet on and watched him climb on the bike. "We'll see about that."

"Want to make a bet?"

If I was betting with Finn, then I was in way over my head. "Sure. What's the bet?"

"If I win and you love the burgers…you have to spend the whole day with me next weekend, watching movies."

Please. I'd purposely lose just to spend the day with him. I better make an equally enticing deal for if I hated the burgers. "Deal. And if I win and I still prefer McDonald's, you teach me how to ride the bike."

He shook his head. "Hell no."

"Then no deal." I leaned in and ran my finger down the side of his cheek and lingered at his jaw. His eyes lit up at my touch, smoldering and hot. I wanted to run my hands through his light brown curls, but I resisted the urge. Barely. "I bet you would've won."

He captured my hand in his, holding my palm against his skin.

"Damn right I would, Ginger. The bet is on. Now climb on and hold on tight."

I got on the motorcycle behind him, my heart still racing from earlier when he'd held my hand close. The look in his eyes did weird things to me. "Don't I always?"

"Yeah. My favorite part of the ride is feeling you plastered against me."

My breath caught in my throat. "What?"

He revved the bike, not bothering to answer. I clung to him as he sped down the road, obviously in a hurry to leave the shady part of town far behind us, but even over the whirring of the engine…

I heard him laugh.

CHAPTER NINE

Finn

Almost a week later, I leaned against the tree and watched Carrie through the window, firmly in stalker mode, as requested by her father. She sat in the library with Cory. The senator had done a background check on him, and he'd gotten the Daddy stamp of approval. He was probably picturing all the perfect little grandbabies he could get out of the perfect little couple already. What a picture they would make on the campaign poster.

I hated the fucking kid for being so perfectly suited for Carrie. Plus, he sat too close to Carrie all the time, and Carrie smiled at him too much.

I sighed and leaned my head back against the tree, closing my eyes. All I wanted was a cold beer and a good game to watch. I was fucking beat. I was getting pretty damn tired of following Carrie around. Not because I didn't like her, but because I liked her *too* much. It's not like she needed me supervising her all the time. It was Friday night, and she was studying instead of partying. Besides the few parties she'd gone to, she'd been remarkably tame. Well-censored with a good head on her shoulders.

She didn't need me. Didn't need Big Brother watching.

I had been even more convinced of this fact after I helped Carrie at the soup kitchen last week. That had been a side of her I probably would have been better off ignoring. Just like the sight of her in a bikini. I could have done without that too. Both made me like her even more. Both made me want things I shouldn't be wanting. Things like her in my arms, smiling up at me like I owned the fucking world. I liked when she looked at me like that. No one else did.

She leaned over and pointed at some nerdy-looking guy's page, her hand gesturing wildly while she explained something to him. The guy looked like he'd never had a friend in his entire life, but Carrie had drawn him under her spell. Cory watched with a disgusted look on his face, but Carrie was oblivious to that. She was too busy smiling at the tiny nerd to notice.

That was Carrie. Loving and accepting of everyone—even a liar like me.

I glanced down when my phone lit up in my hand. It was Carrie. I looked up, checking to see if she was still in the library. She was. So…she was texting me while studying with that Cory kid?

I looked down at her text. *Surfing tomorrow?*

I smiled. *It's supposed to rain.* I tapped the phone against my chin. *Movie marathon at my place? You owe me my winnings.*

She picked up her phone and smiled. *Deal, but that's not fair. It's a bet you knew you would win. Pick me up at ten?*

Hell yeah I did. I never make bets I'll lose. See you then.

Before putting my own phone away, I jotted off a quick text to let her father know that she was in the company of Golden Boy, and then I slid the phone into my pocket. As she came out of the library with Cory, she laughed and swatted his arm. The nerd was with them. She hugged him goodbye and promised to call him next week to hang out. Looked like I needed to do another background check.

Once the gleeful nerd walked away, Cory sighed and pulled Carrie to a stop. They stood at the end of the path, where the boy's dorm went to the left, and Carrie's to the right. If I had to watch her kiss another guy, I wouldn't be responsible for my reactions. I couldn't have her, but I didn't want anyone else to have her.

Yes, I knew how horrible that sounded. I didn't care.

Cory crinkled his nose. "What's with the new guy?"

"I don't know. He seems nice. Why?" Carrie asked, seeming confused.

"Word has it he's an orphan with no one who loves him."

Carrie flinched as if she'd been hit. "Aw, the poor guy. I can't even imagine what he's been through."

"But—"

"No buts. He's nice and I like him." She stared Cory down. "I think I'm going to head up now. Thanks for the study session."

"Want to come to the party over there with me?" Cory asked, pointing behind him. "It's supposed to be fun."

"No, thank you. I have plans already."

She did?

"All right." Cory hugged Carrie close. "Good night."

"Night."

Carrie headed to her dorm room alone, and I breathed a sigh of relief. I didn't want to watch her drink herself stupid tonight. I wanted to drink *myself* stupid, in my quiet, empty apartment. Cory mumbled something under his breath as he passed me, and then headed toward the party raging a few buildings down.

My phone buzzed, and I took it out of my pocket as I headed toward my bike. *Want to start our movie fest tonight? I'm in the mood for a sleepover…*

My eyes went wide. *You want to have a sleepover? At my place?*

Barely a second passed before she replied. *Why not?*

I could think of at least ten reasons "why not" off the top of my head. Every single nerve in my brain shouted no. Screamed it was a bad idea. Even so, I typed: *Sure. Be there in five.*

I waited the required time and walked up to her dorm door. Or, the one she *showed* me was her dorm door. She stood there, wearing the same outfit she'd had on earlier but holding a bag on her shoulder. "Hey."

I caught my breath at the sight of her, her eyes shining as she smiled at me. I swore she got more beautiful, more irresistible, each time I saw her. I took her bag from her and slung it over my own shoulder. "Hey, yourself. How was your night?"

"Good. Marie is at a party, so my dorm was quiet for once. I studied with Cory until a few minutes ago since we have our first exam on Monday, but he went to the party. Now I'm with you."

Thank motherfucking God for that. "So, I'm not your only friend anymore?"

"I guess not." She lifted a shoulder. "I don't even know if Marie is my friend. I think we just kind of deal with each other. We get along and all, but we're really different."

I'd say so. I had seen Marie come out of at least three different guys' rooms during the week, but hadn't seen her crack open a book even once. "Yeah. Not all roommates are instant friends like in movies."

"I guess not." She stopped at my bike. "I like her, but she's not my friend. Not like you are."

I swallowed hard. "Not like Cory, either?"

"Cory is nice. I like him."

"There's that word again. Nice." I flexed my fingers on her bag. "Future boyfriend material?"

She stole a peek at me and her cheeks went all pink. "I have no idea. I'm not really into planning out that portion of my life. If I find someone I like, it'll happen. Until then, I'll focus on my studies, and keep my lips to myself."

I tried to ban the memory of her mouth on mine from my memory. Tried to forget how much she'd seemed like she liked me as she moaned into my mouth. I failed. Miserably. "That's a very mature way to think of it."

"If you say so. I just call it common sense."

I sat down on the bike and handed her the helmet I bought for her. She looked at me with wide eyes, as if no one had ever bought her a fucking present before. "Did you buy this for me?"

"I did." I shrugged and slammed my own helmet over my head, more to hide from her scrutiny than anything. I liked having her on my bike, so I bought her a helmet. Nothing more to it than that. "If you're going to be riding with me, it makes sense for you to have one."

"I'll pay you back." She pushed the helmet down on her head. "How much was it?"

"I don't want your money." I booted up the kickstand. "Now hold on tight."

"But—"

"Just close your eyes and relax."

I revved up the engine, bringing the bike to life. I waited for her to argue, like usual, but she didn't. And when she wrapped her body around mine, laying her head on my shoulder, *I* closed *my* eyes. For a second, I pretended she wasn't my boss's daughter or my assignment. Pretended I wasn't lying to her, and that she wouldn't hate me when she found out the truth. For a brief second, I let myself enjoy the way she felt pressed up against me, her body all soft and willing.

I inhaled deeply, memorizing her scent. She smelled amazing, even when fresh out of the ocean. It haunted me daily. *She* taunted me daily, without even trying. I wanted her.

Too bad I couldn't have her.

I opened my eyes and pulled out onto the road. I took my time on the ride there, taking as many back roads as possible for the short ride. This was the only period I got to feel her arms around me without feeling guilty as hell about it. The only occasion I was permitted to touch and be touched. If I had my way, we'd drive around all night long.

But I didn't.

When I pulled up at my place, I killed the engine and sat there for a second, not moving. Interestingly enough, neither did she. As if by some unspoken agreement, we held each other. It wasn't until a truck drove by that either one of us moved. She dropped her arms from around my waist and removed her helmet.

I took mine off too and our gazes clashed.

She was so beautifully off limits that it hurt. Her hair was sticking up, she had no makeup on, but she looked abso-fucking-lutely perfect. She licked her lips and didn't drop my gaze. "Thank you for the helmet," she said softly. So softly I almost didn't hear her. "And the ride."

"Don't mention it," I said, my voice gruff.

I slid off of the bike and offered her my hand. I should stop doing that. As a matter of fact, I should take her home right now, before I proved myself unworthy of trust—hers and her father's. But sending her away now would only hurt her feelings, and the last thing I wanted to do was that. She would hate me once she found out who I really was.

I didn't want to hurry the inevitable along.

She slid her fingers inside of mine, her fingers so small and dainty, and I held on tight. Right or wrong, I didn't want to let go. I wanted to hold her close, cherish her, and continue to show her how fun life could be when you spend your time with the right person. I wanted to show her *everything*.

"Why are you so quiet?" she asked, darting a quick look at me. "Is something wrong?"

Shit. How long had I been quiet? "No, nothing's wrong." I led her up the walk toward my small studio apartment. "I'm just tired."

"Oh. Do you want to cancel?"

Yes. "No." I unlocked the door. "It's nothing a little bit of coffee won't help."

"No beer tonight?" She nudged my arm.

"Not for the nineteen-year-old. Your father would kill me if he found out I was giving alcohol to a minor."

"You don't know him and he doesn't know you." She rolled her eyes. "I think you're safe."

My heart squeezed tight. "Not if he has security watching you like you said." I hated this game. I hated lying. I hated not telling her *I* was the security watching her. "I'm not going to jail for supplying a minor with booze."

She huffed. "What's the good of having a friend who is older than twenty-one if he won't get me drunk?"

"I'll tell you what I'm good at," I said, stopping and slinging her over my shoulder. "I'm good for surfing, riding a bike, and carrying your cute little ass around."

She giggled and tried to squirm free, but I tightened my grip on her thighs. I liked her in this position. I had a great view. "Put me down!"

"Nope." I juggled her weight and my key, finally managing to open the door to my apartment without dropping her on her perfect little ass. "I'm keeping you forever. Tell your bodyguards that, nice and loud."

She snorted. "If they're watching, they'll come running."

"Then this is a good way to find out if they're here. Play the part of damsel in distress properly." I slapped her ass and stood on the threshold. "Call out for help, or I'll smack you harder."

"Help!" she cried, her voice convincingly strained. "Someone, help me!"

"Nice." I slammed the door behind us and set her on her feet, even though I didn't want to. She rushed to the window and peeked out. "You should get into acting."

"No one's coming. I can't believe it," she said excitedly. "He actually trusted me enough to send me here alone."

Guilt slammed into me, hard and fast and merciless. "See? You were worried about nothing."

"Words cannot describe how happy I am right now that you offered to be my guinea pig." She turned and flung herself at me, hugging me tight. "So I'll show you instead."

My arms closed around her, and I held her close to my chest. I could feel her heart beating fast against mine, as if she'd just caught a huge wave and rode it through to the end. "Hey, now, it wasn't exactly rocket science."

"Still." She rested her cheek on the spot right above my heart. I forgot how short she was until times like this. She didn't even reach my shoulders. "Now I know I can really relax. No one's watching me. You have no idea how wonderful that sensation is. At home, I'd wake up and find security officers watching me sleep. As if a man was going to break in and ravish me in my sleep or something. I had no freedom. None. But now I do, and it's fabulous."

"Your dad had people watch you *sleep*?"

She averted her face. "Yes."

I swallowed hard. I hadn't known that part. That went beyond loving parent and into loony-toon territory. "I'm sorry. That's insane."

"Yeah, that's my dad for you." She lifted her head and smiled up at me, her eyes sparkling. "But I'm finally free."

She was so easily tricked. So gullible. And I was an ass for taking advantage of that innocence. My throat threatened to close up on me and kill me, right then and there in my own apartment. At this moment, I felt that it would have been a well-deserved death. "Right."

She pulled back a little bit, her hands resting on my shoulders, and looked up at me with those big blue eyes. If she kept looking at me as if I owned the sun, I would die trying. After holding my gaze for what seemed like an eternity, she rose up on her tiptoes and didn't stop until her mouth was a scant inch or so from my ear.

"So…since no one's watching…"

I tightened my grip on her. If she suggested we have wild, crazy sex on the balcony…I wouldn't say no. I was too weak right now. "Yeah?"

"How about that drink?"

I swallowed a laugh. I didn't know if I was relieved or disappointed she didn't want crazy balcony sex. "No way."

"We've quite clearly established there is no one watching. That was your excuse."

I dropped my hold on her and removed her hands from my shoulders. "You're just using me for my age, aren't you? Admit it."

"That and your bike." She cocked her head and put her hands on her hips. "Plus, you surf. That's nice too."

"I'm hurt." I held my hand over my heart. "Really."

"You're not bad on the eyes either, when you're not being annoying. Unfortunately for you, that's almost never." She headed for my kitchen, tossing me a teasing grin over her shoulder. "Now show me where you keep the good stuff."

I entwined my hands behind my neck and followed her. Since when did I have to be the voice of reason when it came to drinking? I wasn't old enough for this shit. Wasn't old enough or responsible enough to slip into the role of responsible adult for her. And I didn't want to. "You know you can't drink."

"Says who?" She opened the fridge, grabbed two beers, and set them on the counter. "Everyone else on campus is drinking right now. You know it. I know it."

I dropped my hands and scowled at her. She had a point about everyone else drinking in college, but I still didn't want to be the man who got the senator's precious little girl drunk. That wasn't on my job description. Then again, keeping her from having a drink or two wasn't on it either. At least she was in a safe environment with me.

I crossed my arms. "That's not playing fair and you know it."

"Neither is acting like you're my protector. We're *friends*." She struggled with the beer, trying to open it. Her face turned red as she twisted as hard as she could, and she bit down on her lip. "How the hell do you open this thing?"

I sighed and took it from her. With a simple twist, the beer was open. I held it out to her, but caught her gaze. "I still don't like doing this."

"I know."

She rose to her tiptoes and kissed my cheek. She had to stop doing that shit to me. It wasn't good for either one of us. Her soft lips teased me, and it took a hell of a lot more control than I thought I had to not turn my head and catch her lips with mine. It would be so easy to do.

"Do you now?"

She nodded, her lips brushing against my cheek. "But you need to get over yourself, open a beer, and come watch a movie with me."

With that, she dropped back to her feet and sashayed out of the kitchen, her hips swinging and her red hair looking way too enticing. Hell, *she* looked too damn touchable. My fingers twitched, and my whole body screamed at me to chase after her and claim those soft lips. To make her mine in every way.

Yeah. Get over it.

Easier said than done.

CHAPTER TEN

Carrie

I walked into the living room, my heart racing at light speed due to the fact I'd just kissed Finn. It was on the cheek, but still. It was a kiss. I tipped back another sip, cringing at the taste. Apparently, I didn't like beer, but I was beyond caring. I wanted to relax and enjoy my new freedom, and who better to do it with than Finn, the one guy I trusted? The one guy who made me feel like I could trust him, and let go of all my doubts and fears. Let go of my suspicions even.

He made me want to have fun. Be free.

Be someone else entirely.

Someone he could want like I wanted him.

My phone buzzed, and I glanced at it. It was Dad. I ignored the call, then shot off a quick text telling him I couldn't answer because I was in the library. I felt a little bit guilty at the lie…but really. He needed to back off.

When Finn came into the living room, his beer pressed to his lips and his head tipped back, I couldn't tear my eyes away. His Adam's apple bobbed as he swallowed, and he pinned me down with his penetrating stare. He flopped down next to me on the couch and rested his feet on the coffee table.

"What now?" he asked, not looking at me. "Why are you staring me like that?"

"I'm not staring at you. I was just watching you."

I averted my eyes, taking the chance to shove my phone back in my pocket, and inwardly cursed my heating cheeks. I used the time I needed to regain my composure after getting caught staring at him to survey his home. Everything looked way too fashionable, from the bamboo rug to the grey couch. And he had curtains. What kind of surfer dude cared about curtains?

A neatly made, and *huge*, bed sat in the corner of the room. It had a light blue bedspread and the pillowcases matched. Opposite of the bed was the kitchen, and his black surfboard leaned up against the wall next to his bed. His perfectly ironed military uniform hung in the open closet, along with a ton of t-shirts and board shorts. On top of the closet rung, a shelf held a bunch of socks and boxers. It looked so neat and orderly. So unlike Finn.

It looked like he even folded his *socks*. Who did that?

"Did you decorate this place?" I turned back to him. He sat next to me, doing something on his phone. His brow was furrowed and his fingers flew over the screen. "It doesn't feel like…you."

He threw a quick glance across his apartment and shoved his phone into his pocket. "No. It came furnished."

"Ah. That explains it."

"Explains what, exactly?" He looked over at me, his lips pursed.

"It just doesn't seem like the way you'd decorate your house. It's too… girly."

He grinned. "Worried I'm hiding a wife somewhere in here?"

"Maybe." I stood up and crossed the room, stopping in front of his closet. I ran my hand over the crisp cotton sleeve of his shirt, my heart twisting at the thought of him wearing it in battle. "I forget sometimes that you're in the Marines. Why don't you live on base? Do you like it? Will you get sent overseas?"

"Slow down, Ginger. I can't keep up." He stood up and approached me, stopping at an appropriate distance for friends. I couldn't help wishing that for once he'd stop pushing me away and instead pull me closer. "I don't live on base because I don't want to. I hate base housing and hate the barracks even more. Yes, I like it." He picked up a piece of my hair, toying with it. "And yes, I have gone on deployment before, but I haven't fought yet."

When he rolled the piece of hair between his fingers, tugging gently, I shivered. As if he sensed it, his grip on my curl tightened, then he dropped it.

I turned to him. "That doesn't answer my question. Will you get sent over there any time soon?"

I held my breath. God, please no. Just the idea of Finn in harm's way was enough to make me want to hurl. What if he got injured or…no. I couldn't finish that thought. Ever. He wouldn't go over, and he would stay safe. The most dangerous things he would ever do would be surfing and riding his bike.

"I suppose it's likely. I've heard word of my unit possibly getting sent out sometime in the summer." He leaned against the wall and crossed his ankles. He took another swig of his beer, so I did the same. The thought of him going to war was enough to drive me to drink *anything*. "So I guess anything is possible."

I swallowed hard. "I hope you don't go."

"It's part of the job."

"Still."

Our gazes latched, and for once he didn't back off or turn away. "Don't worry about me. If I do leave, you probably won't even remember my name after a while."

I set my empty beer bottle down and smacked his arm as hard as I could. "Not remember you? What the hell is the matter with you? Of *course* I'll remember you." I shoved his shoulders, wanting to hurt him for insinuating I was so flaky I would forget all about him the second he left, but he simply raised a brow at me. "Of *course* I'll care."

He finished his beer and set his down too. "No, you won't. You'll move on with your life and be fine. You'll probably marry Cory and have little Ginger babies."

I smacked him again. Really hard. "You're such a jerk."

"Stop hitting me." He caught my wrist and narrowed his eyes at me. "And I never claimed not to be one, did I?"

I tried to jerk free, but he didn't let go of my wrist. "Good. Because you're a big, fat, stupid jerk."

His jaw ticked. "What are we? Kindergartners? Resorting to name-calling? Should I call you a poopy-face now?" He released my wrist and slid his hand into my hair. "Tug on your hair and pretend I don't like you?"

I curled my free hand into his shirt and pulled him closer. "Go ahead."

"No." But he did bury his hands even deeper into my hair, making my scalp tingle ever so slightly. And then he pulled. Gently. My stomach clenched with need.

I licked my lips. "Why not?"

"Because I'd rather do this."

He lowered his head, tenderly brushing his lips against mine. He kept the kiss so soft I barely felt it, yet it rocked me straight to my core. That something so little could feel so powerful should have scared me, but it didn't. It made me want him even more because it felt so right. I wanted his real kiss. The one where he held nothing back and gave me the passion I so desired from him.

"Carrie," he sighed against my lips, his fingers tightening on my hair. "You're killing me."

That gave me the courage to try for more. To get something more than a chaste peck on the lips from him. He'd taught me what desire was, and I wanted to learn more—with *him*.

"Then let me help."

Rising up on tiptoes, I tried to catch his mouth again. Tried to get him to break his impervious self-control. But he pulled back without giving me a chance. His hands shook as he disengaged himself from my clinging hands, and he looked down at me with heated eyes.

"You can't help me with this," he rasped. "I'll go get you another beer. Stay here."

Without another word, he grabbed our empty bottles and headed off into the kitchen. I wrapped my arms around myself, shivering slightly. I'd thought I had seen desire in his eyes before I tried to kiss him again. I could have sworn he wanted it as much as I did. Obviously, I'd been wrong. I kept throwing myself at him, and he didn't even want me.

I needed to stop being so freaking pathetic around him. And I really needed to stop melting into a tiny puddle on the floor every time he flexed his hot muscles at me and smiled. He only wanted to be friends, and if that's all I could get, then so be it. I would have to take it.

He came back into the room, a full beer in each hand and his mouth pressed tight. "Look, I'm—"

I held up my hand, knowing exactly where he was going. "I know. You don't need to say another thing. Seriously."

"You're upset," he said flatly.

"I'm not. We're friends, nothing more."

He hesitated. "It's not that I don't want to be more. Believe me. I just can't."

"I know. You've told me." I took the beer from him and took a long, hard drink. "Stop worrying so much. It was fun. It doesn't mean we're anything more than friends, right?"

His knuckles went white on his beer. "Right."

"Good. Glad we're on the same page." I sat down and reclined on the couch. Hopefully I didn't look like I wanted to scream and tear my hair out right now. Because I did. "So, what are we watching?"

He stood there for a second, looking at me. Then he crossed the room and sat down on the opposite side of the couch. Much farther than he had last time. The message was clear. He didn't want any more accidental kissing to happen.

Fine. Neither did I.

He flipped through the titles and then hovered over a movie. "*The Hangover*?"

"What's it about?"

He stared at me as if I had sprouted horns or something equally appalling. "You've never heard of it?"

"My father didn't like me going to the movies. He didn't like movies in general. Said they were nothing but goop for the mind. I snuck into one once, but got dragged out halfway through." Why did all of my stories end with "and I got dragged out?" Geez. Maybe I should see a therapist or something. Or become one so I could talk to myself about my messed-up childhood. I read the blurb on the TV. "And judging from the description and rating, he definitely wouldn't have wanted me to watch *this*."

He shook his head and selected the title. "Oh, Ginger, you don't know what you've been missing."

"Why don't you show me?" I asked, issuing a challenge I knew he wouldn't accept. "All of it."

His mouth clamped down tight. "Don't tempt me."

"Maybe I like tempting you."

"No, you really don't. Now knock it off, or I'll show you what I do with annoying women who don't know when to stop."

Was it wrong I wanted to find out exactly what that was?

And was it just me, or was it hot in here? I took another drink, set my beer down, and pulled my oversized sweatshirt off. Avoiding his eyes, I flung it across the room to my bag. Even though I wore a tight black camisole tank underneath, I felt indecently exposed. What if he thought I was trying to seduce him or something?

Was I trying to seduce him…or something?

As I smoothed my hair with my hand, I stole a quick glance his way. He watched me with hooded eyes. Eyes that saw things I didn't think I wanted him to see. Standing up, I walked to my bag and dug out my pink shorts I'd brought to sleep in. Shorts that seemed way too short now, but that's what I always wore to bed. Shorts and a tank top.

Why should I let it bother me now? After all, we were just *friends*.

Lifting my chin, I squeezed past his outstretched legs, brushing against his thigh as I passed. He stiffened and clung to his armrest, his knuckles white. "What are you doing?"

"Changing into comfy clothes." I grabbed the waistband of my pants, preparing to strip down behind him. "Don't turn around. I'm doing it behind you."

He cleared his throat. "Let me guess. Your 'comfy clothes' are the tiny shorts you're holding and the tank top you're wearing?"

"Mmhm."

He dropped his head back against the chair. "Fucking fabulous."

"If you say so." I stepped out of my pants, feeling out of place in his apartment. It was the first time I stood in nothing but my underwear in front of a guy, and he wasn't even looking. Didn't even want to look. "Do you have a problem with my pajamas?"

"No. Not at all." He adjusted himself on the chair and paused the movie at the starting sequence. "But I'm gonna need another drink before we start. Let me know when you're dressed."

I slid my shorts up my legs slowly, enjoying the freeing sensation I felt at being half naked with him in the same room. "You're good to go."

He stood up and turned around hesitantly. Almost as if he was afraid I'd lied about being dressed. His gaze ran over me, sending liquid heat flying through my veins. Why was it that he set me on fire just by looking at me, and Cory didn't even make me the slightest bit warm?

Without a word, he emptied his beer. My full one sat on the table untouched. He gave me a dark look and walked past me toward the kitchen, his stance rigid. "Stay here. I'll be right back."

I settled down into the corner of the couch, stretching my legs out in front of me, and picked up my own drink. When he came back out, two beers in hand, he set them down and headed for the bed. "I still have a whole beer," I said.

"Then I'll drink them both."

"Okay…"

Reaching out, he ripped the blue quilt off and came back to the couch. He spread it out over my legs and settled down next to me. After removing his shirt, he tucked himself in before he hit play. So he was cold…but he took off his shirt. That was a contradiction if I'd ever seen one. "There. All settled."

"Are you cold?"

"Yeah. Sure. Freezing," he mumbled, taking another swig of his beer.

A thin sheen of sweat appeared on his forehead almost instantly after getting under the blanket. "You don't look cold," I said, unable to stop myself from commenting on his strange behavior.

He sighed. "For once, stop questioning everything I do."

He lifted his beer to his lips, his brooding stare never leaving the screen. Though I would have rather spent the night watching *him* watch the movie, I forced myself to pay attention to the antics on screen. And within seconds, I was laughing hysterically.

When I looked over at him about halfway through the movie, he was watching me with a smile. I froze mid-laugh, my heartbeat increasing when our gazes clashed. Maybe it was the way he was looking at me that sent a surge of heat through my veins. He watched me as if…

As if he'd rather be watching *me* than the movie.

CHAPTER ELEVEN

Finn

The next morning, the first thing I noticed was the sun shining through the slats of the living room blinds. The second thing I became aware of was the warm body pressed against mine. My hand rested on the curve of her hip, and my hard cock was touching her soft ass. There was no question as to whose ass I spooned.

Carrie.

We must have fallen asleep during the last movie we'd been watching. What had it been? Something about a haunted house. Carrie had gotten scared, so I'd thrown my arm over her and cuddled her. Apparently, I had proceeded to cuddle her all fucking night long. She stirred in my arms, wiggling her ass. I gritted my teeth and pushed closer, unable to resist. She let out a soft moan and rubbed against me in her sleep. Fuck. If she kept that up, I'd forget all about the rules and stipulations.

Hell, I might just forget them now and blame it on my foggy head. I dropped a kiss to the spot where her shoulder and neck met, then nibbled lightly. She tasted good. So good that I decided to move an inch to the left and taste her there too. Even better.

She let out a soft moan and rubbed against my cock, making me moan. Fuck me. I shouldn't have started this, but now I couldn't stop. I bit down on her shoulder again and palmed her ass. I squeezed hard, acquainting myself with how perfectly she fit in my hand. She should be mine, no matter what her father would say.

She was mine, even if she couldn't be.

Her head rolled toward me, and I held my breath. Had I woken her up? I studied her face for any signs of her being out of dreamland, but she didn't move. She just crinkled her nose and let out a sigh. I gently removed my hand from her ass and ran it down her cheek, memorizing how peaceful she looked when she slept. It was the only time I'd get to see it, so I didn't want to miss a fucking detail.

When my hand slid down her throat, she arched her back and moaned something that sounded a hell of a lot like my name. I froze, my heart racing, and looked up at her again. Still asleep…but she kept squirming. As if…

As if she wanted more, even in her sleep. I let my hand slide over the curve of her breasts, lightly tracing over her perky nipple. Seeing that she was turned on by what I did sent pure need slamming into my gut. I rolled her nipple between my thumb and forefinger, tugging just enough to pleasure her.

While I played with her perfect breast, she drew in a ragged breath and moaned my name. This time I *heard* it. She was fucking dreaming about me as I touched her. That was too much for me to let go of. I knew I should stop. Knew I should get my hands off her, but she needed me as much as I needed her.

Slowly, I slid my hand down her stomach. When I reached her waistband, I pressed my lips to hers, unable to resist a kiss. I kept it light. Almost nonexistent. But even so, she moaned and stirred in my arms. Damn it all to hell…she was waking up. I didn't know whether to be happy or pissed about that.

I pulled back and moved my hand to her flat stomach before she knew what I'd done. She may expect more out of me than I could give, and I couldn't have that. Her eyes fluttered open, her lids heavy with sleep. "Finn?"

"Sh." I pressed a finger to her mouth, wishing she hadn't woken up yet. Now I had to stop kissing her, even though I didn't want to. "It's all a dream."

She licked her lips, and her tongue ran along my finger, hot and moist. The sight of her pink tongue on my skin was almost enough for me to stop giving a damn. I wanted to press my mouth to hers again. Take her. Keep her.

"No, it's not," she argued.

"You always fight me."

Her lips quirked. "You always say stupid things."

I laughed and forced myself to stand up. To let go. "Get ready. We have a tide to catch. Get dressed out here. I'll get ready in the bathroom."

I headed across the room, grabbing my bathing suit along the way. Thanks to my morning make out session, I now sported a hard-on that I wouldn't be able to hide from her. I'd need a few minutes to myself before I was fit for polite company.

An hour and a half later, I watched Carrie ride the wave I'd sent her out on. She stood on the surfboard, her arms stretched out precariously, grinning with pride as she rode the tiny wave I told her to take. I was probably wearing an even stupider, bigger grin than she was. Miraculously enough, she was starting to get the hang of surfing, and it had only taken a tiny bit of practice.

She was a natural.

Too bad I wasn't a natural at this spy business. Every second spent in her company blurred the lines between friendship and assignment more and more. And every time we were together, it got harder and harder to remember all the reasons I *shouldn't* when all the reasons I *should* were staring me back in the face. Like right now. She was everything I would have hoped for in a girlfriend, and then some.

Kind. Giving. Adventurous. Never afraid to try something new.

And I wasn't allowed to have her.

She tumbled into the water, and I hastily dove for her wrist. She could come up on her own, obviously, but I wouldn't be doing my job if I didn't do anything while she struggled to get to the surface. Eh, who was I trying to kid? I didn't find her because I had to, I found her because I had to make sure she was okay. For *me*—not the senator.

Hauling her up to the surface, I said, "Got you."

She spluttered and swiped her red, drenched hair out of her face. "Did you see that? I had it!"

"You did." I couldn't help it. I grinned with pride again. She was an excellent student, and I was having fun playing the part of teacher. "Soon you won't need my help to catch a wave."

"I wanna go again," she said, struggling to get back up on her board.

Though I wanted to refuse, to drag her to the shore where she could rest up a bit, I couldn't find the heart to make her leave. I could feel the excitement bouncing off her, and I couldn't make her stop now. In fact, I reached out and hauled her onto the board by the back of her wetsuit, then helped her paddle back out to the open water.

Once we reached the optimum surf point, I stopped dragging her, and instead dragged a hand through my damp hair. I hadn't been surfing today. Just supervising. And yet, I didn't give a damn. Normally, I'd be itching to catch a wave myself, but watching her have fun seemed to be enough for me.

She squeezed her hair tight and lifted her face to the sky, letting out a contented sigh. "I never thought I'd have so much fun doing something like this."

"Me either," I said before thinking it through. Then again, I *hadn't* expected to have fun watching her surf. But I did. "I mean, surfing isn't for everyone. I'm glad you like it so much."

"I really do," she said, staring off toward the shore.

I scanned the beach, watching all the tiny people walk around. One in particular caught my eye. She wore a green shirt I'd swear I saw Carrie wear last week. "Uh, Carrie?"

"Yeah?"

"Did you leave a shirt out there?"

She blinked at me. "No…why?"

"I see a girl wearing your shirt. I recognize it. It's the one you wore to the soup kitchen last week. I made fun of the color and you said—"

"That green was the luckiest color in the world." She put her hand above her forehead and squinted. "Yeah. That's mine."

"Why is she wearing it?"

Carrie dropped her hand and fidgeted with nothing at all. "Every once in a while, I put a box of clothes in the dorm. Anonymously."

"Why?"

"Because I have too many."

I shook my head. "Every time I think I know everything there is to know about your giving nature, I discover something new."

Her cheeks went red. "It's nothing." She squinted at the shore. "Oh look. Cory's out there."

I stiffened. She and Cory had been spending more and more time together during the week, and that was all well and fucking dandy. But the weekend was supposed to be my time. It wasn't written down and signed in blood or anything, but it had become our thing, and I didn't feel like fucking sharing. "Why's he here?"

"What time is it?" she asked.

I looked at my watch. "Ten-thirty."

"Shit. I was supposed to meet up with him at ten. I totally forgot. It's so easy to lose track of the time out here, isn't it?"

"Yeah, it is." I cleared my throat. "I didn't know you had any other plans today."

"It came up last night. Cory needs tutoring in anatomy, and I offered to help him today." She dipped her fingers into the water. "I told him we'd meet up after surfing, but I guess when I didn't show up, he came looking for me."

"Smart guy like that shouldn't need help in anatomy," I mumbled. "Then again, guys like him always do."

She shot me a look that suggested she wondered if she'd misheard. "Are you upset? I know we normally hang out after surfing, but we have a big test Monday, and I wanted—"

"I'm not upset," I said, shaking my head at her as if I was amused by the mere idea. But I *was* upset. This was my day, not Golden Boy's. "Now get ready, Ginger. Here comes a good one."

She waved erratically, and Cory waved back. Looking over her shoulder, she started paddling in front of the wave. "See ya at the shore."

"I'll be right behind you."

And I would. There was an even bigger wave coming behind hers, and I could ride it out and meet her at the beach. First real wave I would ride all day. As she took off with the baby wave I sent her on, I watched her safely ride it to shore. Once she made it without wiping out, I readied myself for my own ride. As I rode it, slicing in and out with expert precision, I tried not to watch Carrie as she made her way over to Cory on the beach. Once I hit the sand, I purposely took my time walking over to them, watching from a safe distance. She started taking off her wetsuit, and Cory practically convulsed right then and there on the beach.

What a fucking newbie.

He wouldn't know what to do with Carrie if he got her. Carrie deserved someone more experienced. Someone who would know how to make her scream out in pleasure and wouldn't completely miss her clit while going down on her. Someone like…me.

I walked up behind Carrie and started stripping. "Hey," I said, nodding at Cory. "What's up?"

Cory ripped his eyes from Carrie's sleek body for all of two seconds to nod in my direction. "Hello. Nice surf out there, huh?"

"Not too bad." I threw my wetsuit on the sand and shook my hair in Cory's direction, spraying both Cory and Carrie. Carrie laughed, but Cory gave me a death glare and brushed his hands over his dampened Oxford shirt. "Oops. Sorry."

"No worries," Cory said, smiling, but his attention was *still* on Carrie's body. Didn't she see the way Cory ogled her? Did she know how much the boy wanted more from her than mere studying?

Or, my inner voice whispered, *maybe she knew it and liked it.*

"You should go surfing with us sometime," Carrie said, her voice muffled from under her short blue sundress she was pulling over her head. "It's so much fun."

I snorted. "I don't think Cory is the surfing type."

"I *beg* your pardon." Cory looked down his nose at me, and I stiffened. "I don't expect someone like you to know what I do or do not like, thank you, so kindly refrain from voicing your opinions."

Oh, hell no. No one looked at me like I was gum stuck to the bottom of their shoe and walked away without getting well acquainted with my knuckles. Not since kindergarten. I tightened my fists and advanced on the little fucker. "Oh yeah? Want to know what I do know?"

"No." Carrie pressed a hand to my chest and I stopped. Just like that. The girl held way too much power over me. "I don't think Cory meant that as an insult. Did you, Cory?"

"Of course not." Cory smiled again, just as falsely as the last time. I still wanted to punch him, just as strongly as the last time. "No harm meant, man."

"My name's Finn. Not man."

I looked down at Carrie's hand, which still rested on my chest. My heart sped up at the sight of it, and my vivid imagination ran wild. I pictured her with her hand on my chest, but it wasn't innocent. No, it was while I drove her insane with need. My body buried deep inside hers as she cried out my name over and over again.

That was more like it.

I should kiss her right now, in front of this little jerk. Stake my claim.

"Sorry." Cory held up his hands and backed away from me. *The boy has a brain after all.* "Finn."

"Okay, I'm ready to go." Carrie gave me one last warning look, then bent to grab her board and suit. "You ready to head back to the dorms?"

I clenched my jaw, knowing a dismissal when I saw one.

"Sure. Here. Let me carry that for you. See ya later, Finn," Cory said.

He reached out and tentatively took her board from her, holding it out as far from his perfect pink shirt and plaid shorts as he could get. So she let Cory carry her board, but wouldn't let me? What the fuck did that mean?

"Later," I said, my voice rock hard.

Carrie looked at me over her shoulder, hesitating. "I'll call you later, okay?"

I wouldn't be home. I'd probably be out getting blasted to try to forget how stupid she was making me act lately.

Carrie waited for a reply, but when it became obvious I wouldn't be giving one, she walked off with Cory. As I watched, Cory threw his arm over Carrie's bare shoulders, hauling her close. Her musical laughter came back to me, making me grit my teeth. I'd never wanted to punch someone as much as I wanted to punch Cory right now—and he hadn't even done anything *wrong*.

In fact, he was the perfect match for someone like Carrie.

While I was not.

A few beers later, I leaned back on the bar and took a long pull of my beer. I'd spent the last three hours watching football and was slightly buzzed. For the first time in a long while, I felt free to relax. Free to chill. I knew Carrie was safe. She was with Golden Boy, and he wouldn't harm her.

Hell, he couldn't even get enough balls to kiss her.

Someone tapped my shoulder, and I turned around. A brunette with huge—and obviously fake—breasts sat beside me. She was gorgeous and totally my type. "Hey there."

I tipped my beer at her. "How's it going?"

"Good." She sidled closer, running her fingers over the tattoo on my bicep. "Better now that I've met you."

I should be turned on right now. I *should* be wanting to bring her back to my place so I could fuck her brains out until I forgot all about Carrie. Until I forgot all about everything. But I felt...nothing. "Is that so?"

"It is." She pressed her thigh against mine and caught my gaze. She had blue eyes, but compared to Carrie's, they were dull and boring. "Wanna buy me a drink?"

I took another sip, trying to decide how best to answer. I'd like to pretend I was attracted to her. Maybe even force myself to pretend she was Carrie, and fuck her in the dark. But it felt as if I was betraying Carrie somehow, even though we weren't and never could be a couple.

"Maybe another night." I pulled out my wallet and tossed some cash on the bar. "I was just leaving."

"Your loss," she called out, her tone seductive.

I shook my head and walked out onto the crowded sidewalk. I had enough to drink that I should have been able to finally shake the hold Carrie had over me. But no. She still had her claws knuckle deep in me, whether or not she knew it. For the first time in my life, I didn't know what to do with a woman. Didn't know how best to solve this issue I had where she was concerned.

A laugh came back to me, and I stiffened. Lifting my head, I scanned the crowd. I slowed my steps when I spotted her. She was, of course, with Golden Boy. Cory stopped walking and hugged her close. From my vantage point, she looked stiff. Cory leaned down and kissed her, and she didn't move out of his arms. Didn't squirm or squiggle or try to break free.

Instead, she kissed Cory back.

I clenched my fists and ducked behind a nearby building, waiting to see if she needed any help. When would she push Cory away? Tell him to fuck off? Apparently never. When she pulled back and smiled up at Cory, her hand over his heart like she'd done earlier with me, my own heart twisted and turned.

Fuck that. And fuck this job. I quit.

I turned on my heel and headed home, red coloring my peripheral vision as I shoved my way through the crowd. I knew I had no right to be angry with her. None at all. I'd been the one to insist we be friends, and only friends. I'd been the one who constantly pushed her away, refusing to admit I wanted her, no matter how hard it had been.

Hell, I had practically given her to Cory on a silver platter. If I was in Cory's place, I'd be doing the exact same thing, only I'd be doing it in private, where I wouldn't have to stop. Fucking newbie.

I unlocked my front door and went straight to my fridge. After pushing aside the wine coolers I kept stocked for Carrie, I grabbed a cold beer and cracked it open. Crossing the room, I kicked off my sandals and ripped off my shirt before reclining on the couch. My gaze fell to the spot where Carrie always sat on our Saturday night hangout. The spot she was supposed to be in right now.

It looked ridiculously empty without her there.

"Pathetic," I mumbled under my breath. "You're fucking pathetic, Coram."

I pulled out my phone and dialed quickly. It would be late back home, but I'd bet Dad was still up watching Conan. After two rings, he picked up. "Hello?"

"Hey, Dad." The TV quieted, but not before I heard Conan. I'd been right. Homesickness washed over me, and I swallowed another swig of beer. "Watching TV?"

"Yeah. Nothing's changed out here," Dad said. "How's it going out in California, son? Enjoying the sun, sand, and surf?"

"You know it," I said, smiling at the enthusiasm in Dad's voice. We'd lived in California when I had been a boy, before Mom had died. Before everything had gone and changed. "I missed this place."

"I know," Dad said, his voice gruff. "And I miss you."

"Speaking of which," I cleared my throat. "How likely do you think it would be for the senator to let me off duty earlier than planned? On a scale of one to ten?

"Zero." Dad sighed. "Why? What happened? Sick of babysitting the brat already?"

"It's not that. She's not a brat at all."

"Then what's the issue?" Something crinkled and Dad munched

down on something crunchy. Sour cream and onion chips, no doubt. "You're back in your home state surfing and getting paid to do it. What's the problem?"

I hesitated. I didn't want to tell Dad how deeply watching Carrie was affecting me. The jealousy. The guilt. The feelings I didn't want to name. "It doesn't really seem like I'm needed here, but I don't know how my suggestion of terminating this assignment would go over with the senator."

"Senator Wallington feels differently," Dad said. "Every day, he checks your updates. Every day, he tells me what a fine boy I've raised. He's even suggested when I retire, I'll be getting double my allotted retirement fund thanks to my son's 'go get 'em' attitude and willingness to please."

I dropped my forehead to my palm. There was no getting out of this now. I couldn't do that to my dad. "That's…great, Dad. Really great."

And it was. Dad could definitely use the added money. Getting double his retirement would let him set up home pretty much wherever he wanted. Live comfortably. Not worry about money or bills or food. And when it came down to it, being in California wasn't half as bad as I had thought it would be. If I could get my emotions under control, and get it through my thick head that Carrie would never be mine, it might actually be enjoyable.

"Is something wrong, son? If you're miserable, I'd rather be fired than get double my retirement fund," Dad said, his tone dead serious. "I'll be fine without it."

No, he wouldn't. Not when I could suck it up and be a man. "I'm fine, Dad." I rubbed my forehead. "I was just being stupid. Homesick, I guess."

"I miss you too, son."

I swallowed hard. "Thanks for the talk. I'm gonna go now."

"All right. Good night, son."

"Night, Dad."

I hung up and closed my eyes. Enough of this shit. Enough wanting and wishing and hoping. I needed to focus on the cold hard truth of the matter. If I fucked this up, Dad wouldn't get his nice, cushy retirement pay off. If I fucked this up, I wouldn't be the only one to suffer. It was time to suck it up and stop mooning all over Carrie Wallington, for Dad's sake.

She was an assignment…nothing more.

CHAPTER TWELVE

Carrie

A few nights later, I hugged Cory good-bye, making sure to keep it friendly and not too personal. He went in for a kiss again, but I ducked my head just in the nick of time. After he caught me off guard last Saturday, he'd been trying to kiss me over and over all week long. Of course, I might be partially to blame for that. I hadn't ended our first kiss right away, and had probably given him the wrong impression.

But I hadn't kept the kiss going because I'd liked it so much I couldn't break it off. Not because it set me on fire in ways even twenty thousand romance novels could possibly describe. No, I hadn't ended the kiss because it hadn't done anything at *all*. Zilch. Nada. Zero. Zip.

No matter how many ways I said it, I may as well have been kissing a poster of a fat, balding man for all the excitement the kiss had given me. But when Finn kissed me…

Now, that was another story all together.

"Good night, Cory," I said, patting his shoulder.

Yep. I actually patted his shoulder.

"Night." He gave me a long, almost pleading, look. "See you tomorrow afternoon for another weekend study session?"

"I'm hanging out with Finn," I said, my tone apologetic. "Sorry."

Cory nodded but looked unhappy. Guilt struck me, but I didn't know the right way to let him know I wanted to be friends and only friends.

Maybe I could repeat the speech Finn had given me. It had worked well enough for him. "No problem. See you Monday."

"Bye."

I headed up the stairs to my dorm, expecting to find the room empty. It was Friday night, after all, and Marie surely had plans. But when I opened the door, I found Marie on the couch, hot and heavy with some guy I didn't even recognize.

Marie opened her eyes mid-kiss and pointed at the door. What was I supposed to do? Sit in the hallway? Marie narrowed her eyes and pointed at the door more emphatically. I slowly backed out and closed the door behind me.

Leaning against the hallway wall, I closed my eyes. Okay. Now what? I could call Cory and hang out with him some more, but I was already struggling to find a way to break it to him gently that I wasn't interested in a relationship with him. That left two other options. Walking around without a destination or even an idea on how long it would be until I could return to my room…or Finn.

Easy decision. I missed Finn anyway.

I headed back outside and called a taxi. I knew I should call him first. Make sure he didn't mind if I stopped by. But what if he told me no? If I just kind of showed up, it would be hard to send me away. At least I hoped so.

Of course, by the time the cab arrived, I was losing my confidence in this decision. And after I paid the cab and started up his walkway, I was ready to run back toward the car, even though it was halfway down the road. His bike was outside, so I was fairly certain he was home, but what if he had company? The kind of company he didn't mind kissing?

I hovered outside of his door, pressing my ear against the cool steel door, listening for the telltale noises of sex. All I heard was him talking. Something about watching "Golden Boy." No one responded, so I could only assume that he was on the phone. That was a good sign.

I swiped my hands over my thighs. Taking a deep breath, I raised my trembling fist and knocked. His voice paused, and then I heard footsteps approach. He opened the door, and my breath *whooshed* out of my lungs. He didn't have a shirt on, like usual, but instead of his normal shorts, he wore a pair of camouflage pants. His dog tags, which I'd never seen him wear, hung off his neck, and his hair was shorter on the sides than it had been the last time I'd seen him. A little shorter on the top, too, but there were still some curls.

He looked like a Marine. The type of Marine that went to war. The thought chilled my blood. War had always seemed so far removed from my own life that I never really thought about it besides the occasional story I saw on TV. I'd never known a soldier or a Marine or anyone who would be in harm's way to keep me safe.

Not until Finn.

"Of course, sir." He clenched his phone tighter and held a finger in front of his mouth in an obvious attempt at keeping me quiet. Was he on the phone with his superior? "Yes, sir." A pause. "I will update you on that status when I return from duty." He hung up and shoved the phone in his pocket. "Hey."

"Hi," I said, biting my lower lip. "I haven't seen you in a while. Or heard from you. Are you…is something wrong?"

…and now I sounded like a desperate girlfriend seeking attention.

"I've been busy." He gestured down his body. "Getting ready."

I nodded. "You look ready to go to war."

"Not quite." He raised a brow at me. "I'm missing a few key components. Namely, a weapon."

"Well, duh." I flicked a glance over him again, my legs going all weak. He was always hot, but wearing his uniform, he was catastrophic to my health. "Why are you wearing that? And why did you cut your hair?"

"Because I had to for drill." He tugged on his dog tags. He still hadn't moved out of the opening of the door or invited me in. In fact, he hadn't even smiled or looked happy to see me. "Are we doing surprise visits now? I hadn't realized we were there yet."

I stepped back and glanced over my shoulder. A couple came up the walkway, a young child at their side. They were talking about not having enough money for food again. I made a mental note to drop off a gift card to a local grocery store at their door. "What's drill?'"

"It's something I have to do the first weekend of every month," he said, his jaw tight.

"O-Oh." I cleared my throat. "Are you leaving now?"

He hesitated. "No, I have to report to duty first thing in the morning. Why?"

"So, I guess we're not surfing tomorrow, huh?"

"No, we're not."

I shifted on my feet, not sure what to say next. He was acting cold and uncaring, and I didn't know how to talk to a Finn who acted this way. I'd obviously made a mistake coming here. "You weren't going to tell me?"

"No, I wasn't." He sighed and leaned against the doorjamb. "I didn't realize I had to."

I crossed my arms. "Well, I'm new to this whole 'friend' thing, but it's kind of common courtesy to let someone know when normal routines will be broken, right?"

I forced a laugh, but it hurt to know he hadn't even been planning on letting me know our usual plans were off. Then again, hadn't I done exactly the same thing to him? Yeah. I had. Just last week. Well, *crap*. I'd been a horrible friend and hadn't even known it.

"Yeah." He cocked a brow, his thoughts clearly along the same lines as mine. I could *see* it in his eyes. "Yeah, it is."

"I'm sorry, okay?" I played with the hem of my shirt. "I'm not the best at this stuff. I didn't realize…"

He studied his nails. "What exactly are you apologizing for?"

"For not hanging out last Saturday after surfing. You're obviously mad, and it wasn't right for me to not let you know about it."

"Nope." He looked up at me with something that could only be described as disinterest. "I'm not mad about that. I got over it quickly enough."

I curled my hands into fists. My nails dug into my skin from the force I used, but I didn't even care. "Then *what* are you mad at?"

"Why do you think I'm mad at all?"

"For one?" I craned my neck to look past him. "You haven't invited me in. Do you already have company?"

"Nope."

"If you're not mad, then why aren't you—?"

"The better question is," he crossed his ankles and checked the time, "why are you here unannounced at nine o'clock on a Friday night?"

"I…I wanted to see you."

"Why?" he bit off, as if he couldn't spare more than a single word on me.

"You know what? Never mind." I brushed past him, muttering, "Good luck this weekend."

"Thanks, Ginger," he said, his voice taunting me. "Don't get lost in the ocean without me. I won't be there to save your pretty little ass."

I froze mid-step, my whole body trembling with frustration and anger and hurt. "You know what?" I turned on him, swinging my fist toward his hard, bare bicep. "Fuck you!"

He easily caught my wrist, preventing the blow. His jaw ticked, and his eyes spit fire at me. "What's the matter? Do you not like being blown off? Well, neither do I."

"I *knew* it. I knew you were mad at me." I tried to yank free, but he didn't loosen his grip. "Let *go* of me."

"Or what?" he asked, clearly daring me to do my worst. "What could a little brat like you possibly do to me that would make me let go?"

I knew one thing he didn't want from me. One thing sure to make him release me. I grabbed his dog tags and yanked hard, bringing him down to my level. He didn't even fight me, probably because he'd been expecting me to hit him or shove him or something else painful. Instead, I melded my mouth to his, kissing him with everything I had.

All of my frustration, anger and yes, *need*, came pouring out of me.

He dropped my wrist and gripped my hips, neither pushing me away nor pulling me closer. Spinning me around, he trapped me between the brick wall and his hard chest. When he tilted his head and deepened the kiss, clearly taking control, I clung to the cool metal of his dog tags. With my free hand, I ran my fingers over his abs. I'd wanted to do that since the first time I saw him.

His muscles clenched, and he rubbed his erection against me, teasing me. Taunting me. God, this was how a kiss was supposed to feel. This is how I *wanted* to feel. And I wanted to find this bliss in Finn's arms. No one else's.

I lowered my hand, brushing against the top of his waistband, and then lower until I reached his penis. He arched into my hand, groaning into my mouth. When I closed my hand over him, marveling at the size and feel of him, he jerked and jumped back from me as if I'd punched him instead of touched him. As if I hurt him, instead of bringing him pleasure.

"Damn it, Carrie," he swore, dragging his hands down his face. When he turned to me with blazing eyes, I flinched. "You just go around kissing anyone you want, don't you? Don't care who or where or when? Or how many of us there are?"

I tensed. "What the hell is that supposed to mean?"

"I saw you," he said. No, *snarled*. "I saw you kissing Cory just a couple of days ago, and now you're here, kissing me?"

My heart ached at the accusation in his tone. And the hurt in his eyes… "I didn't kiss him. He kissed me."

"You looked pretty damned happy about it to me." He grabbed the bannister and looked out at the road, his shoulders tense. "As a matter of fact, you looked like the perfect couple, so I really don't know why you're here with me."

I took a step toward him. If he was mad about Cory kissing me, did that mean he was jealous? And if he was, what did his jealousy mean? "I didn't kiss him back."

He spun on me. "Bullshit. I *saw* you. And you liked it."

"No." I held my hands out, desperate to make him understand why I had kissed Cory. To make him see I only wanted him, not Cory. "I kissed him because I was curious. I wanted to know why he doesn't—"

"I don't care why you did it. Just leave me alone." He started for his door, but I stepped in his path, resting my hand on his chest. His whole body tensed, but his heart raced beneath my palm. "Carrie, move out of the way. I'm done here."

I tilted my head back and met his eyes. "No."

"Go bug Cory. He'll welcome it. I don't." He removed my hand from his chest. "I don't play games, and I don't share."

Finally, the anger came back. Thank God, because I needed its strength right now. "Funny, but you told me you didn't want to be with me. Told me you weren't interested. So how is it *sharing* when you never wanted me in the first place?"

"When you came here and kissed me, it became sharing." He still hadn't dropped my hand, but his grip wasn't harsh or even strong. "I'm not willing to be some man you kiss when the mood strikes, before you go running back to Cory."

"That's not fair."

He squared his jaw. "Tell me, were you with him tonight before you came to me?"

I trembled. "I was, but not like you're insinuating."

"There's no insinuation."

"Sure there isn't." I glared at him. "And I'm Mother Teresa."

"Nice to meet you." He dropped my hand. "Now get the hell off my porch."

He was halfway inside the door before I got up enough nerve to ask, "Do you want something different now? Do you want to be with me?"

He froze, his hand on the doorknob. When he looked back at me, his eyes were open and vulnerable. He looked at me as if he did want more. As if he wanted me. But then he opened his mouth and ruined everything. "What I want doesn't matter. It's not happening. Ever. Go chase after Cory instead of me. He'll let you catch him."

"I don't want him," I whispered. "I want you."

He shut the door in my face, and I was alone. I swallowed back tears and started down the steps. Well, that was it. It was over.

All because I'd gone and kissed him.

CHAPTER THIRTEEN

Finn

After drill on Sunday night, I unlocked my door and kicked it open. My eyes strayed to the spot Carrie had stood when I told her to go chase someone else. Even though I tried not to remember what had happened right in this spot on Friday night, it was useless. She'd been on my mind all weekend at training. Haunting me. Annoying me. Making me wish I'd done things differently from the start.

Now that I was back from training, nothing had changed.

She was still on my mind. Still bugging me, even though she wasn't by my side. What was wrong with me? Since when did I let one little spoiled brat of a girl get under my skin so deeply? I squeezed my eyes shut and leaned against the wall, the silence of my empty apartment surrounding me. But the silence soon gave way to her whispered words—the ones that wouldn't leave me the hell alone.

I don't want him. I want you.

And what had I said to her? I'd told her to spend her time with Cory instead of me. It was better this way. The right thing to do. She would move on to someone more suitable, and I would be safe from ruining everything for Dad's retirement. It's not like I needed to hang out with her to watch over her. That had been my first mistake—trying to become her friend. The second had been kissing her. And the third?

Wanting more from her than grade school kisses.

I banged my head back against the wall. "Idiot."

Pulling my phone out of my pocket, I powered it on. It had been off since Friday night, and I was sure I'd have a waiting text or a thousand from the senator. No sooner did the Apple icon disappear from the screen than my phone buzzed.

Everything okay over there? Have you seen her tonight?

I rolled my eyes. *Just walked in. Haven't gone out yet.*

Do so and report back.

Yes, sir.

Apparently my time to sit around moping had come to an end. Duty called, and I couldn't ignore it. After making quick work of changing out of my uniform, I opened the door and headed out to search for Carrie. It's not like I could text her and ask what she was doing. I'd kind of ended that aspect of our friendship the minute I rejected her and acted like an ass.

I'd have to go over to the dorms and see if I could find her. It was five thirty, so chances were she'd be out and about. Maybe at the library. Probably with Cory. Making golden fucking plans for a golden fucking future.

The whole ride over to the school grounds, I was tense and strung out. I wasn't ready to see her with Cory. To see what I'd orchestrated. I pulled the bike up to the curb and took off my helmet. After scouring the library, I came up empty. Everywhere else on campus turned out empty too, but then it occurred to me what day it was.

Sunday. She was probably helping out at the soup kitchen. Alone.

Son of a bitch.

I jumped back on my bike and took the quickest route to the local shelter. By the time I arrived, the sun was down and I had every intention of hiding in the shadows of the parking lot. Once she got in a cab, I could tell her dad she was fine. But as I pulled up on my bike, she walked out the door. She was pale and her hair was frizzy. Huge bags were under her eyes, making her look exhausted. A family came out of the soup kitchen at the same time as her, and Carrie handed them three gift cards.

The family hugged her and she hugged them back. Carrie watched them walk away with a smile on her face. Once she was alone, she stepped under the streetlight and I saw a thin sheen of sweat covering her skin. She'd worked too hard tonight. Then again, she always did, especially when it came to helping others.

As she reached into her pocket to grab her phone, I swore I saw a shadowy shape move behind her, but it could have been a trick of the light. I tried to sink back into the shadows before it was too late and she spotted me, but she turned my way. At first, she didn't see me, but I knew the exact second she spotted me. Her nostrils flared and she gave me her back. Clearly, she planned on pretending she hadn't seen me.

When she pulled out her phone and started texting or calling someone, I hesitated before I walked up to her. "Hi."

"Are we surprising each other now? I didn't realize we were there," she murmured, still not looking up at me.

Okay. I deserved that. Maybe we weren't supposed to be friends anymore, but I could at least apologize for my bad behavior. "I'm sorry I lost it the other night."

"It's fine."

She still didn't look at me. I shifted on my feet and scanned the dark alley behind her. I couldn't get rid of this uneasy gut feeling that something was back there. "No, it's not."

Finally, she lifted her head. "You're right. It's not, but if nothing else, I now know exactly how you feel about me. So thanks for that."

"No, you really don't." I ran a hand through my hair. "I don't even know how I feel most of the time."

"Well, good for you."

Yeah. She was pretty pissed at me. Well, I'd been pissed at her too. "Thanks, Ginger."

She stiffened. "Don't call me that."

"Or what? You'll kiss me into submission again?"

The glare she gave me should have turned me into nothing more than a pile of ashes. Instead, it made my whole body quicken with excitement. I liked when she played hard to get, damn it. "Go away."

"And leave you standing here all alone in the worst section of the city?" I snorted. "Yeah. Not happening. Where's your cab?"

"Late." She walked past me, her shoulder bumping into my arm. It was probably supposed to be a shoulder bump, but she was too damned short to pull it off effectively. "If you won't take the hint, then I'll leave you."

I fell into step beside of her, my hands in my pockets. This wasn't a good section of the city, and she was playing stupid games. I thought I heard a footstep behind us and spun, ready to protect Carrie, but nothing was there. When I turned around, Carrie had an eyebrow raised and an amused expression on her face.

"Chasing shadows?"

"In this section of town, it's probably not a shadow." I searched the darkness, certain someone or something was out there. "Let's go. Now."

"Not with you."

There it was again. A footstep. A shuffle. I grabbed her elbow. "This is an even stupider move than kissing me. You looking to get robbed or worse?"

She broke free and stumbled backward. "I'm looking to get rid of *you*."

"Well, newsflash. Storming off in the worst section in San Diego isn't the way to do it." I reached for her, but she skirted out of my reach again. "Get on my bike, and I'll drop you off."

"Not happening." She tried to step around me, but I blocked her again. She stomped her foot. Actually stomped her foot. "Get out of the way!"

"No. We need to leave. *Now.*"

Something fell in the alley behind us, clattering against the pavement. Carrie seemed oblivious to the threat, but I wasn't. My entire body knew a fight was coming, and I wanted Carrie far, far from it. A shadow moved behind her as my worst nightmare came to life. A man wearing a black ski mask and a pair of black gloves appeared seemingly out of thin air, holding a knife to her throat.

"No quick movements," he rasped, his eyes on me.

I held up my hands and surveyed the rest of the shadows. Nothing else moved. It looked like the mugger was working alone. "Easy now. We're not fighting back."

Carrie's eyes went wide, and her face ghostly white. "Finn?"

"Just do as he says," I said, keeping my voice calm and soothing, while inside I was ready to rip off this asshole's face piece by piece. The man pressed the knife against Carrie's white skin and I saw red. Lots and lots of fucking red. My heart pounded in my head, and my whole body braced for a fight. "Let go of her right now."

The man laughed. Fucking laughed. "Give me all of your money and jewelry, and I'll think about it. Now."

"*Finn*," Carrie said, her voice soft. I could tell she was seconds from panicking, and if she panicked, there was no telling what this man would do.

"Look at me." When she followed my command, I saw the fear deep in the depths of her blue eyes. It was like pure acid in my stomach. I didn't want to see her look at me like that ever again. I didn't drop Carrie's gaze, making sure I looked calm and collected for her. "Do what he says, babe. It'll be okay."

She fumbled with the bracelet on her wrist, her fingers slipping on the clasp. Once she finally managed to get it off, she handed it to the man holding her. He snatched it up and shoved it in his pocket. Judging from the way he shook as he held Carrie, the money he earned from the sale of the bauble would go straight into his veins. Or up his nose.

His unsteady hand made the knife slice Carrie's throat. It was just a tiny scratch at best, but it made me ready to make him bleed a hell of a lot more. "Let go of her."

"Once I'm done, you'll get her back," the man sneered. He pressed the knife even deeper into Carrie's neck and a tiny trickle of blood rolled down her throat. "Money. *Now*."

I wanted to throttle the piece of shit. *Now*. But I knew I had to set the scene right. I needed to get the threat away from Carrie before I made my move. Then it was game fucking on. The asshat wouldn't know what hit him.

"Here you go," I said.

I took a wad of cash out of my pocket and held it out, waving it around just out of reach. The fucker reached for it, but couldn't quite touch. He extended his arm, letting the knife fall away from Carrie's throat. Bingo. Just what I'd wanted.

Moving so fast the man never saw it coming, I captured his wrist and spun it behind his back. The knife clattered to the ground and Carrie leapt back from it, her eyes wider than ever before. Yanking the guy's arm up behind his shoulders, I kept a firm pressure on him. I wrapped my forearm around the guy's neck in a chokehold, squeezing tight enough to knock the guy out but not kill him.

No matter how tempting it might be.

"Come near her again, and next time you won't wake the fuck up," I snarled in his ear, fury making it hard to keep my grip loose. The thief tried to break free, but went limp in my arms. I let him drop to the ground and took the bracelet out of the guy's hand, then shoved the cash back in my pocket too. "Let's go *now*."

Carrie nodded quickly, taking my hand when I offered it. Neither one of us spoke as we climbed on the bike, helmets on and tension high. She clung to me, so I could feel her entire body shaking. Trembling. She might be in shock. I didn't know if the shock was from my quick reaction to the robber, or the robber himself.

Either way, it wasn't good.

I choked the throttle, speeding down the PCH to my apartment. When we got there, I hopped off the bike and yanked off my helmet. After helping her to her feet, I gently removed hers. She looked at me, not touching me but not moving away either.

"Why did you bring me here?" she asked.

I looked around. Though I hadn't thought it through, I'd brought her back to my place. Leaving her alone was out of the question right now. "I don't want you to be alone tonight."

"Oh." She took a shaky breath, her face still far too pale for my liking. "I'll be fine. You don't have to—"

"I want to," I said simply, making sure my tone left no room for arguments. Though I wanted to rail at her, *scream* at her, I swallowed back my anger. Now was neither the time nor the place to release my frustrations at her actions.

She didn't say anything. Just swallowed hard and nodded.

I brushed her hair out of her face tenderly and her eyes drifted shut. "Are you okay, Ginger?"

"Where did you learn how to do that?" she asked, her voice tiny and soft. "It was…crazy."

"The Marines," I said, swallowing past the huge lump in my throat threatening to choke me. So, she was *scared* of me now. Fucking fabulous. "You know I would never hurt you, right?"

She bit her lip and latched gazes with me. I couldn't read the emotions in her eyes. Fear maybe? "Of course."

"I'm sorry you had to see that." I hugged her tight, resting my head on hers and breathing in her scent. "But I'm not sorry I did it. He could have…you could have…"

She gripped my sides, fisting my shirt, and my stomach clenched. "I know."

Seeing that man holding a knife to her throat had done weird things to my insides. I'd be a fool to deny she meant something to me. Something real and huge and unstoppable. Like a force of nature, only stronger. How much longer could I push her away? How many times could I deny the feelings that were so clearly there before I gave up trying?

She shuddered and buried her face in my shirt. "Just take me up to your place, please."

Not trusting myself to speak right now, I swung her in my arms, carrying her up to my apartment. For once, she didn't fight me. She just lay there, letting me cradle her in my arms. Once we were inside, I sat down on the couch with her still in my arms.

I couldn't hold it in anymore. "That's was the stupidest, most stubborn, idiotic—"

"I know."

"—thing I've ever seen you do."

"I *know*."

"And you will never, ever go there without me again. Understood?"

She swallowed and nodded. "Yes."

Her easy acquiescence did nothing to soothe my temper. I needed a fight. Needed to make her see how stupid she'd been in storming off like that. "If I hadn't been there—"

"But you were," she said quietly.

"But *if* I wasn't." I tightened my arms around her, picturing all the horrible things that could have happened to her. All the gruesome things men liked to do to defenseless women like her. "Do you have any idea what it would do to me if you were hurt? I can't even imagine—"

She lifted her head and kissed me, shutting me up quite effectively. For once, I didn't want to fight her off. Didn't want to give a damn about my duties or expectations. Didn't give a damn what kind of contract I'd signed that said I wasn't allowed to touch her. For once, I…

Didn't want to stop.

CHAPTER FOURTEEN

Carrie

I held on to Finn as tight as I could, kissing him for as long as he would let me. At any minute, he would push me away and curse, but I didn't care right now. After the scare in the street, and his even more impressive saving of my stupid butt, I couldn't stop thinking about how it had felt with that knife to my throat. I hadn't been as scared for myself as I had been for Finn when he went for that guy. I'd been terrified he would get hurt trying to save me.

Frightened he would get stabbed or worse…die.

All because I had to go and be a stubborn idiot who refused to leave with him. I *knew* better than to walk off into the dark city streets. Knew not to storm off in a huff when danger lurked nearby. My actions had put myself, and consequently, Finn, in danger. If he had been injured trying to save me, I never would have forgiven myself.

I strained to get closer, but his hold on me didn't allow me to move. He broke off the kiss and dropped his forehead on mine, taking a shaky breath. "I don't want to stop, babe. I swear it. But you could be in shock…"

"I'm not," I said quickly, grabbing his hand and holding it to my cheek. "I'm fine. I want you so bad it hurts."

His jaw flexed, but I could see his answering need in his eyes. "I shouldn't."

"You should."

"Carrie..." He closed his fingers on my hips, lifting me up and lowering me on his lap so I straddled him.

"Oh my God." His erection pressed against my core, making me moan. I entwined my hands behind his neck, the cool metal of his dog tags digging in to my skin. He hadn't even taken them off before seeking me out. "You really should, Finn."

He made a long sound, half groan and half agreement. "I can't fight this anymore. I don't even want to."

And with that, he buried his hands in my hair and tugged me down, his mouth seeking mine. For that brief second, the time that our mouths hovered close to each other, I knew I hadn't made a mistake in falling for him. I had fallen hard, and there was no going back.

His lips touched mine and all thought fled. All I knew was Finn was kissing me, and things finally felt right. And this time when he kissed me, he held nothing back. I knew it from the way his lips moved over mine. His mouth devoured mine hungrily, and he arched up against me, letting his erection rub where I needed him most. I dug my fingernails into his shoulders, holding him closer.

Begging him not to leave with my actions instead of my words. If he pulled away now, I didn't think I would recover. If he stopped now, I just might break. But he didn't. Instead, he stood up and cupped my butt, holding me in place as he headed toward the bedroom. Slowly, he lowered me to his bed, never breaking off the kiss.

My head spun as his lips worked mine, making everything but him disappear from my mind. The way he kissed me. How amazing his hands felt on my body. The feel of the soft bed underneath my back, contrasting with his hard body on top of mine. Pressing me down and making me want more.

Tentatively, I ran my fingers down his back, sliding them up his shirt when I reached the hem. His hot skin burned my fingers, and the way he moaned into my mouth set me afire. I traced my nails down his spine, growing bolder the lower I went. When I reached the waistband of his shorts, I scraped my nails against his lower back.

He hissed and tore his mouth from mine. "Are you sure you want this?"

Unable to talk, I nodded and reached for him again. He stretched and ripped his shirt off over his head, and then melded his mouth back to mine. His free hand, with the other firmly on my hip, roamed all over. My sides. My stomach. My neck. When he traced the curve of my breast, I gasped into his mouth and arched my back.

He needed to do that again.

Apparently I said that out loud. He chuckled. "I will."

"Please," I whimpered.

Slowly, he crept my shirt over my stomach, stopping at the bottom of my bra. I caught my breath, afraid to move. Afraid if I made a sound, he would grow a conscience again and stop doing those magical things to me. He met my eyes, his own hot and unwavering. "Have you kissed Cory again?"

"W-What?" I asked, caught off guard.

"Since you kissed me, have you kissed him?" he asked, his jaw ticking.

I shook my head. "No. Of course not. Just the once."

"Good." He lifted my shirt a little bit more, his fingers brushing my bare skin, never dropping my gaze. "You're mine now. Don't forget it."

I swallowed hard at the possessiveness in his tone. I should argue or say I didn't belong to any man. Assert my independence. But right now? Right here? I was his. One hundred percent his, and perfectly happy to be there. "I won't. Now kiss me again."

He took off my shirt the rest of the way and closed his mouth over mine. As he worked his magic with his tongue, his fingers toyed with the strap of my bra, tugging gently. Before I could even blink, he had the strap undone and was lowering the tiny scrap of fabric off my breasts. For a second, I worried he might not like what he saw. Worried I would disappoint him somehow.

But he reared back and looked down at me…and I was lost. He was seeing what no man had ever seen before. I didn't want to hide from him. Didn't want to deny him a single thing. Not tonight. I let my hands fall to my sides. He swallowed so hard I could see it, and then traced a finger over my bare stomach, creeping closer and closer to my left breast.

"You're the most beautiful woman I've ever seen," he uttered, almost as if he didn't realize he said it out loud.

Before I could respond, or even decide if I *should* respond, he lowered his head to my breast, flicking his tongue over my sensitive nipple. "*Finn,*" I cried out. I gripped his head, urging him closer. Needing him closer.

His slid his hands under my back, arching my back for me. I bent one leg, spreading my thighs to let him in. Knowing instinctively that he needed to be there to ease the ache building inside me, begging for release. He moved into the crook of my thighs, but didn't press his erection against me. Instead, he scraped his teeth against my nipple and sucked harder.

"I-I need you." I licked my lips and added, "Please."

His hands trembled as he let go of me and undid my pants. I lifted my hips, letting him undress me, and didn't so much as flinch as he lowered them down my legs. When he reached for my panties, I grabbed his hand and swallowed the nervous bubble of laughter threatening to escape me.

I might be a virgin, but I knew what came next. And before I was completely naked, things needed to get taken care of. "Do you have protection?"

He pushed off the bed and opened the nightstand next to it, pulling out a purple foil package. He tossed it onto the bed and made quick work of removing his shorts. When he ripped off his boxers, I didn't drop my gaze from his body. If he saw my shyness and my uncertainty, he might back down. As it was, he surely thought I was more experienced than I was.

I knew if *he* knew I was a virgin, this wouldn't be happening.

As he stepped out of the last piece of clothing he wore, I feasted my eyes on him. Tattoos covered his upper arms and shoulders. That I already knew. But his lower half was devoid of any ink. In a way, I was glad. The perfection of his body was an artwork all by itself, and I couldn't help but think any more ink would detract from the muscle and flawlessness I saw right now.

When my gaze dropped to his penis, I practically choked on the deep breath I took. No matter how many romance books I read, I hadn't been expecting *that* much length. Holy crap. No romance book could ever have prepared me for this. He was magnificent.

He approached me, his steps sure. When he lowered his body over mine, I stopped trying to do calculations on the likelihood of him fitting all the way inside of me without tearing something vital. I wasn't a fool. Women had been doing this since the beginning of time, and I was no different than any of them.

Though Finn might just be bigger than all the other men.

He sucked my other nipple into his mouth, ripping open the condom as he did so. After a few quick movements, his hands were back on my skin, burning paths everywhere he touched. My blood heated, and my stomach clenched tight, building a pressure that I was powerless to stop. Powerless to control.

When he kissed a path down my stomach, taking little bites as he went, I went mad with desire. Tossing my head back and forth on the pillow, I moaned and cried out and dug my nails into his skin. He flicked his tongue over my clitoris before taking that into his mouth too.

Oh, holy mother of freaking God. That felt way too good to ever stop. I would make him stay down there forever. He could take breaks for water and food, but that was it. I dug my heels into the mattress, letting out a whimper that didn't even remotely sound like me.

He groaned and adjusted his hold on me. I, in turn, tightened my legs on his head, refusing to let him move until he gave me what I needed. Until I found the release I knew his mouth could give me. "Don't stop," I demanded, panting for air.

He ran his hands up my calves, then down my thighs. When he reached my hips, he lifted me higher. Something in the changed position must have made for optimal pleasure, because my whole body tingled and went weak. I clung to his hands, needing to hold on to something secure before I let go of all control.

And when I did, letting the pleasure wash over me, all of the pressure that had been building inside of me burst into a million pieces. As my whole body went limp with gratification, he dropped my hips and settled in between my legs. He rubbed against me, exactly where his mouth had just been, and another wave of intense pleasure crashed over me.

Capturing my face in between both of his hands, he kissed me gently. As his mouth played over mine, I could taste the familiar flavor of Finn I'd come to know and also myself on his tongue, making for an intoxicating combination that made me even more eager for him to come inside me. More desperate for him to fill me completely.

"Carrie," he gritted out, his hold on my hips tight. "I can't go slow or be gentle."

I opened my mouth to warn him about the technicality of me still being a virgin, but it was too late. He thrust inside of me with one quick movement, and the pain of him ripping through me blended with the satisfaction at having him buried deep inside of me, where I'd wanted him for weeks.

CHAPTER FIFTEEN

Finn

Having Carrie in my arms was more than I could bear. Better than I'd imagined. Nothing could describe the way she made me feel, so I wouldn't even bother to try. I fused my mouth with hers before surging into her, unable to believe how fucking amazing she made me feel. How she could bring me to my knees with a simple touch. Make me want to stay there too, I'd bet. I'd had sex with a good amount of women during the years, but I'd never done this.

Never made love before.

But then I crashed through the resistance I'd suspected might be there. I reared back, looking down at her with concern. "Are you okay?" Then, realizing I should act surprised, I added, "Wait. You're a virgin?"

"Y-Yes." I started to pull out of her. She closed her legs around my waist, blinking back tears even as she tried to keep me inside of her. But I was *hurting* her. "No. Don't stop. I want…I need…"

She rolled her hips up tentatively, more than likely experimenting with the sensation of having me inside her. I gritted my teeth and forced myself to remain still, letting her test out the waters, so to speak. "You should have told me."

"I was afraid you'd stop," she said, running her fingers lightly over my back. "Please don't stop. Don't let go."

"I've got you," I promised, nibbling on her ear. I knew I should stop.

Should end this right here and now, but she kept moving underneath of me, and letting out tiny breathy moans that drove me fucking wild. I couldn't stop. Not ever. "And I won't."

She thrust her hips up again, and a sheen of sweat formed on my forehead. Her tight pussy gripped me more closely than I could ever have imagined, and my cock screamed at me to move inside of her. To finish what I started.

She dug her heels into my ass, urging me closer. "It doesn't hurt anymore. Move inside me."

I pulled almost all the way out of her, then slowly drove back in. I groaned at the pleasure she gave me, unable to bite it back. Her body fit mine like a glove. It was as if she was made for me and me alone. My arms trembled from the strength I exerted to hold myself back. To not hurt her. I kept my weight on them, not wanting to crush her. "That okay?"

She nodded and lifted her head. "Kiss me and move faster."

The control I'd had over my motions snapped, and I crashed my mouth down on hers. I moved inside of her, hesitantly at first, but growing more and more sure as I went. She moaned and squirmed beneath me, begging for more. Once I was certain I wasn't hurting her, I lifted her hips in my hands and drove deeper. She cried out and scratched her nails down my back, probably drawing blood and waking up the neighbors.

I didn't even give a flying fuck.

I needed her too badly. It had all started with an immediate attraction, but now it was more. So much more. As I grew closer and closer to the precipice, I tried to focus on her. The way her eyes were slit, barely letting me see the bright blue sapphire. The way she let out tiny puffs of air through her swollen lips. But most of all, the way she moaned my name as I brought her higher and higher, refusing to stop until I made her come again.

When she finally tensed and bowed against me, frozen in time, I let myself go. I thrust one more time inside of her, going as deep as I could possibly go, and cried out, "*Carrie.*"

As the strongest orgasm I'd ever had rushed through my veins, I collapsed on top of her, keeping my weight on my elbows. She tightened her legs around me, seeming to not want to let me go, and hugged me close, her own breathing as ragged as mine. If she didn't want to let me go, that was fine by me. I could happily lie here as long as she wanted me to.

I buried my face in her neck, closed my eyes, and waited for the regrets and the guilt to come. Waited for cold, hard reality to come crashing over me once I remembered all the reasons I shouldn't have done this. And even more terrifying? Knowing she would hate me for taking her virginity while lying to her. When she knew what I really was—*who* I really was—she would never forgive me for taking her under false pretenses. And I would never forgive myself either.

I needed to find a way to fix this.

I lifted myself on my elbows and looked down at her, sweeping her sweaty hair off her face. I knew I should be feeling that suffocating guilt right about now, but it wasn't coming. She smiled, her eyes warm and soft and on me. "Wow."

"Yeah." I grinned at the wonder in her voice, despite myself. "You okay, Ginger?"

She nodded and arched a brow. "Are *you* okay?"

I laughed. "I think so." I slowly withdrew from her, watching her for any signs of pain. She flinched when I pulled out of her completely, but besides that she seemed fine. "You really should have told me, though."

She didn't even pretend to misunderstand me. She was a smart girl, my Carrie. "Would it have made a difference?"

I thought about it, but I already knew the answer. I wouldn't have stopped. I'd been lost in her the second she walked out on that beach more than a month ago, demanding for whoever was hiding in the shadows to show themselves. I'd been lost this whole time, but I'd been fighting it. I was done fighting her. From now on, I would fight *for* her.

For us.

"No, it wouldn't have. I couldn't have stopped any more than you could have," I admitted. "But now I need to take care of you."

I brushed my lips over hers before sliding off the bed. As I walked to the trash can to remove the condom, I took a deep breath. This *obviously* changed everything between us. I couldn't ignore my need to be with her any more than I could ignore the pressing need to admit my real identity to her before it was too late.

She would be angry with me at first, but if I came clean on my own—without her finding out when I wasn't there—then maybe she would understand. Maybe she could find it in her heart to forgive me and allow us to continue on as we had been, only without any lies between us. Yeah, and maybe some pigs would fly by wearing Wonder Woman costumes too.

Actually…that might be more likely.

I turned around and crossed the room to my bed. She let out a squeal when I picked her up and carried her into the bathroom. "I can walk, you know."

"You can, but I want to carry you." I kissed the tip of her nose before I set her down in front of the shower. "And you like making me happy, so you'll let me."

She huffed. "So, that's how you're gonna play this, huh?"

"Uh-huh." I turned on the shower, grinning the whole time. I couldn't remember the last time I'd felt so happy. Probably never. "Is it working?"

She splayed her hands over my shoulders, sliding them in front of my body. She rested them over my heart, pressing her cheek against my bare back. "Yes." I stopped moving, not wanting to break her hold. Not wanting her to let go. But then she did, and she slid her hand under the water. "Perfect. You coming in, too?"

I cocked a brow. "You have to ask?"

She laughed. "Guess not." She stepped into the shower and smiled at me. "This is weird. I've never showered with someone else."

"Well, it's another first for you then." I joined her and pulled her into my arms. Her naked body pressed against mine, making my cock harden again, but I wouldn't touch her. Not tonight. She needed rest. "I want to be all your firsts from now on."

She laid her head against my chest, directly over my heart. Did she know she owned it yet? "Sounds like a plan."

I grabbed her hair and got it damp, watching the water cascade down her bare back, only to roll down her ass. After clearing my throat, and mentally slapping myself in the face for being a perv, I reached for the shampoo. As I washed her hair, her eyes drifted shut and she let out a happy sigh.

I rinsed out the suds, watching her face as I did so. She looked so peaceful and innocent. "Sorry, I only have men's shampoo."

"That's okay." Her lids drifted up. "I'll smell like you."

I made a mental note to buy her some girly shampoo in the morning.

And a toothbrush. If I had my way, she'd be spending a lot more time here with me from now on. "Next time, you'll have something better."

Her eyes drifted shut again and she yawned. I made quick work of washing her body, pausing at the blood smeared between her legs. I'd done that. Taken her innocence. The fact that she'd chosen me, trusted *me*, was enough to make me want to scream. Soon, she would hate me. Soon, she would regret this.

I rinsed her off, and then quickly washed my own body. She leaned against the tile wall, her eyes devouring me. "Can I do you?"

I bit back a groan. "I don't think that's a good idea. I already want you again, but you can't handle that. Your body needs rest."

She licked her lips. "Are you so sure of that?"

"Yes." Fuck my fucking conscience. "Positive as a proton."

Her eyes went wide, then she let out a nervous laugh. "You heard that?"

"I did," I admitted, shooting her a sheepish grin.

"Oh God." She dropped her forehead onto her palm. "How embarrassing."

"You mean adorable?"

"Nope," she quipped.

I turned off the water and grabbed two towels. As we dried off, my eyes never left her. She was so gorgeous. Her pale skin contrasted fantastically with the smattering of red curls between her legs. She had a few freckles across her body, but for the most part, she was all ivory skin and temptation. I dropped my towel and cupped her face, tilting her it up to mine.

I ran my fingers over the line of freckles that ran across her cheeks and over her nose. "I love these little freckles. You know that?"

"I hate them."

"They're perfect, just like you."

I kissed her, making sure I kept it light. I swung her in my arms and carried her to the bed. After I gently set her in the middle of it, I reached down to the foot of the bed and lifted the covers over her bare body. She lay on her side, her hands folded under her cheek, watching me. I pulled my phone out of my pocket and quickly let her father know she was safe and sound.

I just neglected to mention she was safe and sound *in my bed*.

When I crawled under the blanket with her, she smiled and ran her fingers through my damp hair. Something that had nothing to do with lust rolled over me, like a tidal wave. She nibbled on her lower lip and tugged the blanket higher. The pink tinge in her cheeks hinted at her vulnerability.

"Stay the night with me?" I asked.

She gave me a small smile. "Do I really have a choice? You already tucked me in."

"Not really." I pulled her into my arms. "I was simply pretending to be a democracy."

She snorted, but burrowed closer. "Fine, but are you going to wake up and then curse and apologize in the morning?"

"Nope." My arms tightened around her. "I'm done fighting."

She smiled up at me, her eyes shining. "Really?"

"Really."

She smoothed a piece of my hair off my forehead. "So, uh, are we still just friends? Or…?"

I laughed and hauled her against my body. "Some friends might do that, but not me. We're more than friends now, Ginger."

"Do we have a name?" she asked, her voice soft.

Yeah. Mine was *liar*. Hers would be *mad*.

The guilt I'd been expecting had arrived right on schedule.

But for one simple night, I didn't want to think about anything. Didn't want to think about repercussions, or what her dad would say when he found out I hadn't followed the rules. Even worse? What *my* dad would say. Would my actions ruin Dad's chances at getting the big retirement pension?

No, I couldn't let it. I'd find a way to fix this, but it started with telling Carrie the truth.

"I'm not sure yet, but I know this changed everything," I said, kissing the top of her head. "Every fucking thing."

Her fingers closed around my shoulders, holding on tight. She yawned loudly. "You don't exactly sound happy about that."

"I'm happy." I swallowed all of my fears and doubts, trying to drown them out with a bright smile. "I have you. What more could I need?"

"How was drill?"

"Boring and utterly exhausting." I hesitated, then added, "And I missed you."

"I missed you, too." She smiled and snuggled into the crook of my elbow. "Can you wake me up at seven for class?"

"Yep."

I reached out and switched off the light. I lay there, holding her close, and tried to come up with the best way to tell her what I was. Tried to come up with a gentle way of breaking the news. Bad thing was? There wasn't one. No matter how I said it, she would hate me.

Her breathing evened out almost immediately, but the weight of my lies pressed me down into the mattress until I couldn't breathe anymore. How was I supposed to sleep when I could think of nothing but what I'd done?

And what I had to do. I had to tell her.

"You awake?" I whispered.

She mumbled something and scooted closer to me, letting off a soft snore. I wanted to wake her up and spill my guts, but I forced myself to lie still.

Tomorrow. Tomorrow I would tell her the truth.

CHAPTER SIXTEEN

Carrie

This afternoon class was never going to end. I sat back in my seat and eyed the clock. Only three more minutes until my class was over, and then I could see Finn. He'd promised to meet me at the dorm afterward, and I couldn't wait to see him again. Couldn't wait to kiss him and hold him and hug him. And, well, more.

I fanned my cheeks with my notebook as I recalled exactly what we'd done last night, and how amazing it had made me feel. How amazing *I'd* made *him* feel. I wanted more. Lots more. I'd known sex brought pleasure. Known I would enjoy it. But with Finn, it far surpassed pleasurable. As a matter of fact, what he did to me just might tip the Richter scale.

Cory elbowed me and tipped his head toward the professor. The professor, meanwhile, was looking at *me*. No. Scratch that. The whole class was watching me. I sat up straight in my seat and smoothed my hair. Why were they all staring at me?

Professor Hanabee turned red and shoved his hands in his pockets. "Would you be answering my question anytime soon, Carrie?"

"Uh," I said, looking to Cory for some help. He didn't even look at me. Just stared at the front of the classroom. "What was the question again?"

The professor rolled his eyes. "Cory?"

Cory gave the answer easily.

I looked down at my notebook. All I'd done was draw squiggles and a few random words like *bilateral* and *hemorrhage*. I thought I saw Finn's name in there too, but I could be wrong.

Professor Hanabee gave me one last, piercing look, then turned back to the class. "There will be a quiz tomorrow. You may go now."

While everyone else got up, I kept my head lowered. My cheeks were on fire, but I knew that I had no one to blame but myself. I'd always been at the head of my class. Straight A's. Eye on the end game. What the heck did I think I was doing, neglecting my academic obligations to daydream about a guy? I slammed my book shut and stood. After collecting the rest of my stuff, I started down the steps.

"A moment, please?" Professor Hanabee called out.

"Yes?" I climbed the rest of the way down and stood in front of his desk.

He wore one of those god-awful professor jackets with the patches on the elbow, and his glasses kept sliding down his nose. He jammed them back up with a short, stubby finger. "Did I mention I'm friends with your father? He calls for updates every so often. I'd hate to give him a bad answer."

I swallowed hard to stop the scathing reply trying to escape. Of *course* Dad would have friends on staff. He had spies *everywhere*. "Yes, sir."

I headed for the door, mentally figuring out how much time I would need to cram a day's worth of missed lesson into my head. Would there still be time for my fun evening with Finn? Could I do both? Cory waited at the door for me, his sandy blond hair perfectly in place like usual. The complete opposite of Finn's messy curls. He leaned against the wall, phone in his hand.

When I came to his side, he lifted his head. "Hey."

"Hey." I scanned the crowd for Finn. "Sorry about today."

He followed my gaze. "Looking for someone?"

"Yeah," I answered distractedly. "Finn."

"Marie said you didn't come back to the room last night." Cory shoved his phone in his pocket and gave me a look. A look that said he had his suspicions where I had been, and what I'd been doing. "Where were you?"

I stiffened. "I don't see how that's any of your business."

"I thought that we had something going between us, so, yeah, it kind of is."

Cory yanked on the collar of his polo. His pink-and-yellow striped polo, buttoned all the way up to his neck. Did he ever let loose? Wear a T-shirt that didn't come from a brand name store, or stop thinking so much about what everyone would think about him if he did?

"We're just friends. I like you a lot, and you're a great guy. Excellent, really. Any girl would be lucky to have you." I sighed. God, I sucked at this stuff. "But I'm kind of with someone else right now."

He stiffened. "The surfer?"

"Yeah." I swallowed back my arguments that Finn was more than a surfer. More than what Cory decided to label him as. He was smart, funny, handsome, brave…

Cory chuckled and his shoulders relaxed. "Good."

I blinked at him. "Good?"

"Yeah." He stared at his impeccable nails. "It won't last, and when it falls apart, you'll come back to me."

"That's a really shitty thing to say," I snapped, heading toward the doors. "He's a great guy."

Cory's mouth pressed tight. "He can be great all he wants, but it still won't work. You aren't the same type of people."

"You're wrong." I stopped walking. "You don't know him like I do."

"No, I'm not wrong," he said, his face red. I opened my mouth to slam his opinions to the dirt, but he didn't give me a chance. "You've got plans in your life that don't include a surfer boy who has no immediate goals in *his* life besides when he should catch his next wave."

"He has a great job. He's a Marine." I took a breath. "How dare you pretend that's not a career."

Cory rubbed his temples. "He's got nothing to offer you, really. Can't help you study. Has no knowledge of what you'll be doing with your life. Won't get along with your father. He's a rebellious stage in your life. Nothing more."

"I don't *need* him to help me study. I'm fine on my own."

"Sure you are," Cory agreed, nodding. "But that's not the biggest problem. The biggest problem is that you two have nothing in common. The things you like about him now? The stuff you think you admire most because he's so different?" Cory leaned in, latching gazes with me. "That's the stuff that will make you hate him later."

Could he be right? Would I eventually hate Finn's laid-back lifestyle? His quest for fun? The way he laughed as he surfed, his eyes lit up and his laugh blending with the sounds of the waves crashing on the shore? "You're wrong."

"No, I'm not. I learned it in psychology." He nodded his head toward the dorms. "Speaking of the devil…"

Finn came up to my side and cleared his throat. He wore a light yellow shirt with a surfboard on it and plaid shorts. His shades were firmly in place, and his short curls were a little messy. Not messy enough, though, due to his haircut. "I was starting to think you forgot about me."

"No. No, of course not. I'm just a little bit late because I got in trouble."

"You?" Finn raised a brow. "How could *you* have gotten in trouble?"

"We'll talk about it later." I knew I should get ready for the quiz tomorrow, but I didn't want to give up time with Finn. I could make time for both. "Come on."

Finn took my hand and nodded at Cory. "Later, Cody."

"My name's Cory," Cory said, his voice hard. "But you already know that, don't you?"

"I have no idea what you're talking about," Finn said, his tone completely innocent.

Even I believed him…almost.

Cory grabbed my arm as we passed, and Finn stiffened next to me at the touch. "Are you going to study?" Cory asked.

"Yeah. Later."

Cory flexed his jaw and let go of me. "Fine. See you later."

"What was that all about?" Finn steered me toward his bike.

"Nothing. We have a quiz coming up. I'll study later tonight."

He stopped walking and looked over his shoulder at Cory. "Are you sure? Your grades come first. Maybe you should go with Golden Boy."

Golden Boy. Why did that name ring a bell? I shook my head, shaking away the niggling sensation that I'd heard those words before. "No, I'll be fine. You promised me cheeseburgers and milkshakes, and I intend to collect."

He wrapped his arms around me and tugged me close. "First, you need to pay up."

He lowered his mouth to mine, giving me a passionate kiss that quite literally knocked the breath out of me. I curled my hands into his shirt, trying to urge him closer, and he moaned before breaking off the kiss. Before I could so much as blink, he slid the helmet over my head and reached for his.

"I've got a surprise for you."

I bit down on my lower lip. "Oh? What is it?"

He sat down on the bike and looked straight ahead before slamming on his own helmet. "You'll just have to wait and see."

CHAPTER SEVENTEEN

Finn

I pulled the bike up to the curb and closed my eyes, relishing the way her arms felt around me. Loving the fact that I could show how much I liked it when she clung to me, now that we were together. Now that she knew how I felt about her. I tore my helmet off, and then picked her up, setting her on my lap.

She shrieked at the sudden movement and flung her arms around my neck. Her sweet ass pressed down on me, making my cock hard, but I wasn't looking for that right now. I just needed to hold her because I fucking could. "Hey, babe."

I gently removed her helmet and set it aside. The way she looked at me…

I loved it.

I could get used to seeing that same light shining in her eyes for the rest of my goddamned life. And that's what I wanted. Not a short period of her life. I wanted forever. Even though I knew, subjectively, that we were doomed from the start. I'd started this relationship with lies, and it would end the second the full truth came out.

And even if I hadn't lied to her, she was too young to even contemplate forever. A baby, practically. When I'd been nineteen, the furthest thing from my mind had been love or settling down with someone. To her, this was nothing more than the obligatory college fling.

"Why are you looking at me like that?" she asked breathlessly.

I snapped myself out of whatever unicorn land I'd been stuck in. "Like what?"

"Like I bit you or something."

I snorted. "You can bite me anytime you want, babe."

She slapped my arm, but I barely even felt it. She was like a mosquito bite on my arm. "Keep it up, and I just might. And I bite really hard."

"I hope that's a promise."

She rolled her eyes. "So is this the surprise? I already knew you had an apartment."

I chuckled and nuzzled her neck. "That's not the surprise."

"Then what is?"

She arched her neck to allow me better access. Nice. I nibbled some more. "You'll have to go in and find out."

She hopped off my lap and practically ran up to the door. *Note to self: she likes surprises.* I followed her more slowly, grinning at her exuberance. When she turned to me impatiently, her hand out, I set the key in her hand. She burst inside the door—and then stopped.

She scanned the room, looking for any signs of something different. Turning to me, she cocked a brow. "Uh, where's the surprise?"

"Right here."

She eyed me, her eyes dancing. "Is it you?"

"I wrapped something with a bow."

Her gaze dropped to my cock, and her voice came out breathy. "Seriously?"

I burst into laughter. "Nope."

"Darn, that would've been fun."

I made a mental note to remember the idea. "It's better than that." I reached into her bag and retrieved the item I needed. I brandished her anatomy book with more flair than I knew I had in me. All for the greater good, of course. "We're spending the night...*studying*!"

"Studying. Really," she said dryly. "I can hardly contain my excitement."

"I see that," I said, laughing. "But that's not all."

She perked up. "Oh? What else?"

"Every time you get an answer right, I get to kiss you anywhere I want." I let my gaze dip down low. "And I've got a few ideas where I'd like to start."

Her cheeks flushed and she licked her lips. "And if I get it wrong?"

"Then you don't get kisses and you go home with Cory to study."

"I thought you hated him."

I gently shoved her down on the couch and laid my body on top of hers. "I do." I nibbled on her ear, biting a little bit harder than necessary. "So you better get the answers right."

She dug her nails into my shoulders. "Fine, but I need time to study."

"Time granted." I gave her a long, searching kiss, my tongue circling hers. When she kissed me back without hesitation, her body melding into mine more completely than her mouth, I almost forgot her need to study. Almost forgot part of my job was to make sure she didn't get distracted from her duties.

I was distracting her, and I had to stop.

With a groan, I pulled back and ended the kiss. "No more of that until our studying session starts." Hopping to my feet, I handed her the textbook and headed for the kitchen. "I'll be out on the patio, cooking you dinner."

She blinked up at me. "You cook?"

"Hell yeah, I cook. Better than that, I *grill*. I have one on the back porch." I gave her a cocky grin. "I'm more than a pretty face, Ginger."

"I already knew that," she said gently, meeting my eyes. "In fact, I knew it as soon as you opened your mouth and told me about yourself."

I froze. I had been mostly joking, but I'd dealt with the assumptions I was nothing more than a pretty boy with no goals all my life. Hell, right now I was playing the part of that exact type of person. She saw the real me? Knew I had goals and aspirations?

I cleared my throat and forced myself to stop standing there like an idiot. "Uh, good. Now off I go. Study hard, woman. I don't want you hanging out with Cory."

She laughed and cracked open the book while I set about getting ready to grill some burgers outside. But first, I pulled the vanilla ice cream out of the freezer and grabbed some milk. I scooped half the container into the blender, added milk, then threw in some Oreos for good measure. I had promised her a milkshake before realizing she had to study, and she'd damn well get it.

I switched the blender on, and she looked up at me. When she saw what I was making, her eyes went wide. After I switched off the blender, she said, "You make milkshakes too?"

"Yep." I pulled two red cups out of the cabinet. "And they're the best you'll ever have."

"Really?"

I emptied the contents of the blender into the glasses and stuck two straws into the cups. "See for yourself."

I crossed the room and gave her the glass with more in it. She took it from my hand, her fingers brushing mine as she did so. She wrapped her perfect lips around the straw and closed her eyes. And I was jealous of a fucking straw. "Holy crap, you're right."

"I know I am." I grinned. "Now get back to studying, or I'm taking it back."

She hugged it to her chest. "Never."

Her phone rang and she dug it out. "Hello?" Silence. "Yeah, of course I can help you. How about tomorrow after class?" More silence. "Sure. I'll see you then, Keith."

Keith. Who the hell was Keith?

She hung up and smiled at me. I arched a brow. "Should I be worried about this Keith guy?"

"Nope." She pushed her hair out of her eyes. "Remember the guy Cory was mean to?"

Nerd boy. "Yeah."

"He asked me to help him plan the booth the school is running at the Relay for a Cure taking place next week." She set down her phone. "I told him to contact me if he needed help. His parents died of cancer…and so did your mom. So I wanted to help."

I swallowed hard, moved by her compassion. "That's nice of you."

"It's nothing at all," she murmured distractedly, taking a sip of her milkshake. "I wish I could do more."

Her attention was on her book, so I left her alone. She was always so busy wishing she could do more that she didn't see she was doing enough. Her heart was big enough to encompass everyone around her, including me. I headed back into the kitchen, sipping my own milkshake. As I sliced the tomatoes and onions, I kept stealing glances at her. She sat on my couch, completely silent with her head bowed over the book, and

I couldn't get my mind off how much I liked this little bit of domesticity. I could get used to cooking while she studied.

And I could *definitely* get used to helping her study.

Hopefully when I told her the truth later tonight…it wouldn't be a thing of the past. I just wanted to let her study before the fighting began. Or so I kept telling myself.

Though studying hadn't been in my plans for the night, I hadn't missed the way she'd hesitated when Cory asked her if she wanted to study. I knew she was torn between doing what she *wanted* to do, and what she *should* do. Hell, I knew that particular dilemma all too well. So I made the decision for her. She could have both. She didn't need Cory to study.

She had me.

I might not be going to college to become a doctor, but I could certainly hold up a flashcard and help her cram words into her head. When I finished cooking dinner, I headed back inside. She was still on the couch, but she'd sprawled out across it and was balancing the book on her chest. I set the platter of burgers down on the kitchen counter, cracked open a beer, and took a long draw, my eyes on her the whole time. She'd finished her milkshake. Maybe I'd make her another one later. Anything to make her happy.

Her mouth moved silently as she read, but otherwise she was still. Yep. I definitely could get used to this. "Dinner's ready."

She jumped slightly and looked at me. "What?"

"Dinner." I motioned to the plate behind me. "It's ready."

"Oh." She set the book down and rubbed her temples. "I didn't realize I'd been reading that long."

"Yep, you were."

I stood in front of her and tugged her to her feet. She wrapped her arms around me once she was standing, then kissed the spot directly over my heart. I hugged her close, my heart speeding up at the soft kiss. I wished…

Wished these things would never change. Wished she wouldn't have to hate me. Wished I didn't have to tell her the truth tonight. The cowardly part of me wanted to hold back. Wait. But I knew it was the right thing to do, even if I didn't want to.

She rose up on tiptoes and kissed me. "Ready?"

Hell no. "Yeah, come on."

I grabbed her hand and led her into the kitchen. As we built our burgers, mine with mustard and ketchup, hers just ketchup, I kept stealing glances at her. She was tapping her foot as she created her meal, her lips moving silently. I had no idea if she was singing or citing medical terms, but either way…fucking adorable.

I grinned. "You singing a song over there?"

"Hm?" Her foot stopped mid-tap. "Maybe."

I scooped her up in my arms. "Don't stop. I love it."

Her cheeks tinged pink. "Really?"

"Really."

She pushed out of my arms and tucked her hair behind her ear. "Well, then, you better get used to it. I'm kind of a dork."

"I find you adorkable."

She snorted. "That was a pretty adorkable thing to say."

"We have to stick together."

She flopped down on the couch. "I have to eat this, then give me ten more minutes to study." She picked her burger up. "Then we play."

"Deal."

We ate in companionable silence. Once she was finished, I cleared our plates and busied myself with the dishes while she studied. I leaned against the counter and dried my hands. "How's it going over there?"

She glanced up at me. "I feel like I ate a house, but I think I'm ready."

I crossed the room and took the book out of her hands. I glanced down at the page and scrunched my eyebrows together. "Exciting stuff, huh?"

"It's anatomy." She stretched her arms over her head, baring a tiny strip of stomach. That was all I needed to want her. Hell, I didn't even need that. "None of it is exciting."

"I beg to differ," I said. I dropped to my knees in front of the couch and pushed her shirt back up. She sucked in a deep breath and held it, her bright blue eyes on me. "I find anatomy, yours in particular, quite exciting."

She arched a ginger brow at me. "Oh really?"

"Mmhm." I ran my fingers over the bare strip of skin and kissed it. "Really."

She threaded her hands through my hair, holding me there. I closed my eyes and practically purred like a cat. This. Right here. I could live like this quite happily for the rest of my life. I nibbled on the patch of skin right under her belly button, tightening my grip on her hips when she started squirming.

"Don't stop doing that," she whispered, her eyes drifting shut. "Like, ever."

I didn't want to. "Are you sore?"

"No." Her cheeks turned red, and she opened her eyes to peek at me. "My lower extremities are fine."

"Look at you, showing off your medical vocabulary." I kissed her stomach, this time a little bit lower and grabbed her waistband. "Say something else the book taught you, and I'll kiss you again."

She spouted off some medical jargon I couldn't really understand, but it sounded legit. As long as I got to kiss her some more, I'd be happy. I undid her pants and pulled them off her legs. She had a dark purple satin thong on that just might be my favorite color in the whole world right now. I ran my fingers over the soft satin, dipping down to brush across her clit.

Her left leg fell to the floor, granting me better access. I took full advantage of this, slipping in between her legs and nibbling on her upper thigh. "Say something else or I'll stop."

"The way you make me feel..." she moaned. "Will soon cause a series of muscle contractions in the genital region...that will be accompanied by a sudden release of endorphins."

I blinked up at her, amusement threatening to overtake my desire. "Did you give me the medical definition of an orgasm?"

"Yes," she said through her teeth. "Now kiss me again."

I laughed and flicked my tongue over her clit, through her panties. "More."

"Argh." She yanked on my hair with just enough force to make my scalp sting. I liked that too. "When the endorphins rush to my head, I'll experience a sudden sensation of..."

I tugged down her panties, listening to her medical talk, but not really paying attention. At this point, I was a little bit too distracted by the fact that I wanted to make those endorphins she'd mentioned rush to her head. Repeatedly. When her thong fell to the floor along with her pants, I nibbled my way up her thigh. The closer I got to her clit, the faster she babbled. And the faster I forgot all about studying, and could only focus on her.

She whimpered and tried to urge me closer. I let her take control of me. Let her put me where she wanted me…but only because I wanted to be there. When I flicked my tongue against her clit, her legs jerked and she moaned. I liked the sounds coming out of her mouth. I needed more.

I rolled my tongue in a lazy circle, keeping my touch light. She dug her nails into my scalp and lifted her hips, begging for more. Her soft scent teased me. She smelled like lilies and something else. Something fruity and intoxicating and *her*. I gripped her hip with a trembling hand, holding her in place, and slipped my other hand in between her thighs. She said she wasn't sore, but I wasn't about to thrust inside of her without making certain of that fact.

I swirled my tongue a little harder this time, then gently slid a finger inside her. She was tight. Too tight. My cock ached to be buried inside her slick folds, but I ignored it. Her muscles clenched down on my finger, hard, and I increased the pressure of my mouth a fraction more.

"Don't stop, don't stop," she panted, over and over again, her nails digging into any piece of skin or scalp she could reach. She'd apparently given up on medical lingo. "*Finn.*"

As soon as she said my name, I pulled out and put another finger in, my tight hold on control slipping fast. I needed her too badly. Power like this wasn't good. Wasn't right. Yet, she held it over me without even trying. And worse yet? I didn't think I stood a chance at breaking free because I didn't even want to.

Her muscles clamped down on me, and she froze, her entire body rigid and held taught. Then she breathed my name again and collapsed to the couch, her breathing erratic. I stood up and crossed the room, going to the nightstand to grab protection. As I approached her, I undid my shorts. Her cheeks were flushed and her hair was messy. She looked fucking hot right now, right after I made her come.

She sat up and licked her lips. "Can I…can I do that to you?"

"Fuck yeah, you can." I kicked my shorts off and let them fall to the floor. All of the contents of my pockets spilled on the floor, but I didn't give a damn. All that mattered was *her*, and making her happy.

She reached out and trailed her fingers over my abs, her touch feather light. I closed my fists, nearly crushing the condom in the process. This might be the most torturous thing I'd ever put myself through, but it just might be the most pleasurable too. She pulled me closer, and I stumbled forward, letting her put me where she wanted me.

When I stood between her bare knees, she looked up at me through her lashes, almost as if she tested my reaction before she even started. I slit my eyes, making it look as if I wasn't watching her, but I'd be dead before I missed the sight of her mouth on my cock. She leaned in and flicked her tongue against the tip of me, and every muscle in my body jerked in response.

"Hm," she said, shifting her weight on the edge of the couch. She cupped my balls gently, running her fingertips over the sensitive skin. I hissed and tightened my jaw. She was going to kill me with her almost-there caresses. "Do you like that?" she asked, her tone throaty and whispery and oozing of sex.

"Yes," I managed to say through my swollen throat. "Do it again."

She grinned and rolled her tongue over the head of my cock, this time doing a complete circle. I'd tried to keep my hands to myself, but she broke my restraint. I dropped the condom on the floor and buried my hand in her red curls. I urged her closer, gently, in case she changed her mind.

She didn't.

Without warning, her mouth closed around me and she sucked me in, keeping the suction constant and the pressure *just right*. I looked down at her, watching her fuck me with her sweet red mouth, and couldn't look away. Each time she drew back, she took more of me in. And she didn't stop playing with my balls, increasing the pleasure by tenfold. My fingers flexed on her head, and I forced myself to stand still. To not thrust into her warm mouth…but it was the hardest thing in the world to do.

To just stand there, while I wanted to bend her over and fuck her senseless.

When she sucked me in more, making me grow horribly close to an orgasm, I placed my hands on her shoulders and pulled out of her mouth. My entire body tensed when she increased the suction, trying to keep me in, but I refused to come in her mouth. I needed to take her gently and sweetly. I needed to make love to her the way I would have if I'd known it was her first time last night.

"No more," I rasped.

"But—"

"*No*. If you keep doing that, I'll come." I ran my finger over her hard nipple, squeezing gently. "But when I come, I'll be buried deep inside of you. I won't accept anything else."

I ripped open the condom and slipped it on before bending down and carrying her to the bed. After laying her down gently, I lowered my body over hers and kissed her. She wrapped her arms around my neck and tentatively slid her tongue between my lips. It was the first time she kissed me like that, taken the initiative during sex, and the devastating effect it had on me was not missed.

My arms tightened around her, and I wished I could hold her close forever. Keep her safe forever. Make sure no one ever hurt her again. But *I'd* be the one hurting her. *I'd* be the one ruining the very thing I so cherished…her trust.

She curled her legs around my waist and lifted her hips. "Now," she demanded.

After taking a calming breath, I slowly inched inside of her, making sure to be gentle. To go slow. My body shook with the effort it took to hold back, but it was worth it. She deserved this and more. When I pulled out and moved inside of her even slower, she broke free of our kiss and looked up at me.

"What's wrong?"

I gritted my teeth when she dug her heels into my ass. "Nothing, babe."

"Then move." She arched her hips up while slamming her heels into my ass, and I surged inside of her another few inches.

Still, I held myself back, even though the sweat pouring down my forehead was stinging my eyes. "I…don't want to…hurt you."

"You won't." She cupped my cheeks and smiled up at me, her eyes shining with tears and something else. "I trust you."

I swallowed hard, the guilt threatening to overwhelm me. To choke me. I needed to tell her the truth. Now. "I have to tell you something. I'm—"

She curled her hands behind my neck and jerked me down, kissing me passionately. When she arched her hips up, taking me completely inside of her, I groaned and pressed even farther in. She increased the pressure of her lips, her teeth digging into my lower lip, and moved again.

136

"Carrie, I—"

"Tell me *later*," she demanded against my mouth. "I need you. Harder."

And that? That was my undoing.

I pulled out of her and thrust inside, sure and fast. She moaned and scratched her nails down my back, so I repeated the gesture. As I moved inside of her, something inside of me gave way, and I knew I would never go back to the way I'd been before her.

Her legs clamped around me even tighter, and her breathy cries grew quicker. She was close. So close. I reached down between us, never breaking the kiss, and pressed my thumb against her clit. She moaned into my mouth and pumped her hips up once, twice, then came—her body tensing all around me. I slid out of her and drove back inside, my own orgasm taking control of my body within seconds of her release.

I collapsed on top of her and buried my face in her neck. Taking a deep breath, I tried to remember the last time I'd felt this way after sex, but I came up empty. I had never felt so damned happy and satisfied after sex until…until Carrie.

I couldn't lose her. Not now. Not ever.

CHAPTER EIGHTEEN

Carrie

Now *that* was what I called a study session. I closed my eyes and took a nice, long breath. No matter how many times I read the why and how of sex, nothing compared to the reality of it. The reality of Finn touching my bare skin, moving inside of me and taking me higher and higher…

Yeah. Nothing.

I shivered and within seconds he had a blanket over me. He was always so considerate and compassionate. I shivered, he got a blanket. I yawned, he got me to go to sleep. I needed to study, he kidnapped me and forced me to do so. He was supportive, hot, and honest.

Cory didn't have a clue what he was talking about.

Finn was everything I wanted in a partner and more. I wouldn't grow to hate him for his "faults." Heck, I had yet to *see* any faults at all. Surely he had some, everyone did, but he hid them well. He stood up and headed for the trash can as I watched. The back view was almost as enticing as the front.

Almost.

He turned on his heel and scratched the back of his head. He always did that when he was nervous. I knew that about him. Why would he be nervous?

"You want another milkshake now?" he asked, his voice uncharacteristically hesitant. "We can sip on them while we finish studying."

"I already got my reward." I sat up, bringing the blanket with me. "What possible reason do I have to study now?"

He raised a cocky brow, and just like that, the Finn I knew was back. "Your grades? Your father? Your whole life?"

"Eh." I shrugged. "I like your methods of persuasion far better than those."

He grinned and crossed the room, then bent down to give me a lingering kiss before pulling away. His hand remained on my neck, his touch gentle. "Then far be it for me to leave you hanging. I'll go clean up, but we need to talk. Deal?"

"Talk? That sounds serious."

"Nah. It's just something I have to tell you." He gave me a lingering kiss, but seemed as if he didn't want to let go. As if something was wrong. "I'll be right back."

He gave me one last look before he headed into the bathroom, closing the door behind him. I let out a little sigh and slid out of the bed. As much as I'd like to remain here all night, he was right. I had studying to do, and I wasn't about to do that naked. I got dressed in my clothing, but couldn't find my shirt anywhere. When I spotted his red shirt lying on the floor, I grinned and slipped it over my head.

It smelled like him. Delicious.

As I hugged the shirt close to me, I caught sight of his phone lying on the floor under the table. I reached down and pulled it out, intending to set it down on the table so he wouldn't be looking for it later, but right when I picked it up, the screen lit up. I tried not to look. I really, really did. It's not like I wanted to be that girl who snooped through my boyfriend's phone for hints of other women in his life. And yet…

My gaze flitted to the closed bathroom door before it returned to the phone in my hand, and what I saw there made my heart stop and my stomach twist in tight, painful knots. As if the floor dropped out from underneath me, letting me crash to my death five hundred feet below. At first it was the all capital letters in the text message that drew my attention. Dad texted in all caps, as did most older people. But then I looked at the number, and my entire body went all weak and shaky with disbelief. Confirmation came swift and hard, like a kick in the stomach. I'd know that phone number anywhere.

I read the text again.

Have you seen her today? Is she studying with Cory?

For a second, I hoped I picked up the wrong phone. That I held my own phone in my hand, and not his. That would be so much better than the alternative. So much better than knowing that the first person I trusted enough to let get close to me, the first man I could possibly see myself falling in love with, was nothing more than a spy sent by Dad.

Oh my God. I was such a fool. I'd fallen for it all, without even questioning why a guy like Finn would want me. Without a second thought or a backward glance. Now I was staring the truth in the face. Dad was texting Finn, and Finn was hanging out with me because he *had* to, not because he *wanted* to. He'd been sent here to babysit me, and I'd been dumb enough to believe he might actually be interested in me.

That he actually cared.

I blinked back tears when the bathroom door opened, and Finn came out wearing a pair of boxers. "About that talk, how about if we—?"

He scanned the room until he found me, and then he broke off midsentence. He looked first at the phone in my hand, then at my face. He paled and stopped walking midstride. He opened his mouth, closed it, then tried for a casual tone of voice. "You okay, babe?"

Okay? No, I was not okay. I was horrible. Terrible. Ready to cry and scream and kill Dad for doing this to me. For sending Finn to watch me. For sending a man I could so easily fall in love with, then ripping him away from me without a second thought.

And I was even madder at myself for falling for it.

"Was it all a lie?" I asked, my voice miraculously even, even if it came out soft. I slowly lifted my head. "Tell me the truth for once. Was it all a *lie*?"

He flinched and seemed to break out of a trance. He crossed the room and held his hands out in front of him. "No. Please, let me explain."

"*No.*"

I stumbled to my feet and backed away from him. I couldn't bear his touch after all of this. After he…oh, God. No. I couldn't even think about it right now. I tossed his phone onto the couch, not wanting to hold it another second. In some sick way, I almost blamed the phone for all of this. If I hadn't picked it up, I wouldn't be feeling like the world had stopped spinning.

"Carrie, I didn't pretend to like you. It's not history repeating itself."

"Oh my God, you know all about that too?" I covered my face with my hands. Somehow, him knowing all about my embarrassing past made it worse. So much worse. "Did you get a file on me? All my dirty little secrets?"

He flinched. "Yes."

"Unbelievable." I swallowed hard, my head spinning so fast I couldn't even keep up. "I can't believe it was all a lie. Do you have any idea how much I liked you?"

"Please. Let me explain."

My heart twisted so hard it hurt. "Explain what, exactly? How you lied to me to get close to me? How you pretended to care about me? Or maybe how you slept with me because my dad told you to?"

"*No.*" His voice broke. "It's not what it looks like."

"So you're not watching me for my father and reporting back to him?"

He flinched. "I am. But—"

"There are no *buts* in this situation. None at all." I let out a harsh laugh. "God, I'm such an idiot."

"It wasn't all a lie. Not the way I feel about you."

"Don't even go there." I stared at the bed, the sheets still rumpled from our recent bout of sex. Swallowing hard, I covered my face with my hands. My stomach lurched, and I swallowed back the bile threatening to rise. "I can't believe I…we…"

"Carrie, don't think like that. What we did there has nothing to do with your father," he said, his voice raspy. His hand rested on my shoulder. "I wasn't even supposed to—"

I shrugged off his hand and dug my nails into my palms. The pain was a welcome distraction from the stronger, more mind-numbing pain he was causing me. "Don't touch me! I trusted you. Actually *trusted* you."

His shoulders drooped and he held out his hands. "I know. I'm sorry. You have no idea how sorry I am."

"I don't want to hear a single apology." I pushed my hair out of my eyes and shook my head in disbelief. "What you felt or pretended you felt means nothing to me anymore. Just tell me everything from the beginning. How do you know my father?"

"I work for him." He clenched his hands at his sides. A muscle in his jaw ticked, but otherwise he looked completely unaffected. "I was sent here to watch over you because I'm the youngest in the security squad."

"Wait...what?" He couldn't possibly work for Dad. I'd have remembered seeing *him* around the house. "I've never seen you there before. I know all the guys."

"I started working for him while you were abroad. When you came back, the senator hid me. His plan was already in motion," he said, his shoulders straight and his head held high. "I didn't want to do it, but he promised me a higher position and a raise if I stuck it out for a year."

Stuck it out for a year. As if it would be so horrible spending time with me. At least he had found a pleasing way to pass the time for himself. Seduce the senator's daughter and laugh about it after. I swallowed past the tears threatening to escape. "Wow. So you get paid for banging his daughter behind his back. That must be poetic justice, huh?"

"No." He reached for me, but before he could touch skin, I stepped back and gave him a dirty look. His hands fell back to his sides. "It wasn't like that. It's not like that. If he knew what I did, I'd be fired, and so would my father. He works for your dad too."

"Your father?" I eyed him, trying to figure out who his father could possibly be. There was only one man with a son who could be Finn's age, and he was the one I liked the best, of course. "Oh my God. Not Larry?"

Finn flinched. "Yes."

"But his son isn't called Finn. He's Griffin...oh..." I sank onto the couch, my legs trembling. "Oh my God."

"I didn't lie about my name. Finn is my nickname, and I kept my mother's name because she was worried her side of the family would die out. There were lots of Hannigans, but no more Corams." He tugged on his hair and shook his head. "I didn't want to lie to you. I didn't like doing this. I'm sorry."

It hurt enough knowing he'd been lying this whole time. To know that he hadn't really liked me or even cared about me. Hearing him apologize for the farce was too much. "Stop *saying* that."

"But I am sorry."

I ignored him. I had to keep focusing on finding out the why and how, or I would break. I needed cold, hard facts. "How often did you have to report back to him? Did he...?" I paused, scared to ask this next question. Scared of what the answer might be. "Did he tell you to pretend to want to be with me? To act like you were interested in me?"

"*No.*" He dropped to his knees in front of me, his gaze latched with mine. "I swear to you that nothing between us was a lie on that front. Not the friendship. Not the sex. Not a single conversation. I fell for you, and I fell hard. There was no fighting or pretending. None of it was a ploy to get close to you."

"You're telling me that you came up to me on the beach simply because you *had* to know me?" I leveled a look on him and when he flushed I had my answer. "Exactly. Contrary to what I've shown you so far, I'm not gullible."

"I know you're not, but I'm telling you the truth." He looked toward the bed, then back at me. "I care about you, Carrie. More than I care about my job or myself. More than I should ever have let myself care for you."

"Stop saying that," I demanded, covering my ears. I couldn't believe him. Not ever again. "You're a liar and I don't trust you, so just *stop.*"

"I know." He nodded and stumbled back from me, his mouth held taught. "I'm sorry."

If he said he was sorry one more time, I'd scream. Literally scream. I pulled my phone out and started typing Dad's number. This was over right now. "I'm calling him."

"I know." He paled even more. "Go ahead. Tell him how much I fucked up."

I paused with my finger over the screen. He'd said something about his father earlier. If I called Dad, would Larry get fired? "So what happens if I call my dad and tell him I know what he did? Will he send you home?" I hovered with my finger over the send button.

His shoulders drooped and he fell back against the wall. "Yeah. I'm sure I'll be fired, and you'll never have to see me again."

Still, I hesitated. "Why did it have to be a lie? Why you too?"

He took a shaky breath. "Carrie, please." He dragged his hands down his face. "I swear to you I didn't mean to hurt you. I tried so hard not to fall for you. To push you away. But I couldn't."

I swallowed hard. "Are you really twenty-three?"

"Yes."

"Are you really a Marine?"

He dropped his head into his hands and sighed. "Yes." He lifted his head. "I told you, the only lies between us were the fact that I didn't tell you why I was here." His jaw flexed and he pushed to his feet. "The rest is real. I am still your friend and your—"

I laughed harshly. "You're not my friend. You were never my friend. It was all an assignment."

He flinched. "At first, maybe, but not now. Not for a long time."

My heart squeezed so tightly I couldn't breathe. Oh, how I wanted to believe him. How much my heart begged for him to be telling me the truth. But that's exactly why I couldn't. I'd fallen for his lies once. I wouldn't do it again. "Just stop. Stop the act. I'm not standing here so you can lie to me. All I want is information."

He just stared at me. "What else do you want to know?"

Everything. Nothing. What I really wanted was for us to go back in time to a few minutes ago. Back to when I'd been blissfully unaware of the fact that Finn had been spending time with me because he had to.

"How often do you report to him?"

"Every day," he said. "I watch you and report back to him every day. I'm supposed to keep doing so throughout the next year."

I clung to the table next to me, giving him my back. He'd been following me. Studying my motions like some sick stalker or something. All in the name of Dad's twisted need to control me. To control my life. The thought left a sick taste in my mouth. "Why did you let me get this close when you knew it would come to this?"

"I couldn't stop myself." His footsteps crept closer. "I fell for you hard, Ginger."

I whirled and shoved him backward as hard as I could. So hard my palms hurt, but it still wasn't hard enough. I would never be able to hurt him as much as he hurt me. "Don't you dare call me that now. Not ever again. You don't have that right anymore."

"Fine." He didn't back down at all, his eyes flashing. "Go ahead and call it in. Tell your father I failed. Tell him to fire me."

"So he can send another man out here in your place?"

He shrugged, the motions carefree, but the look in his eyes did nothing to hide the tension swirling inside him. "The next one will probably be better at keeping his hands to himself."

I curled my fists. "Unlike you?"

"Unlike me." He met my eyes again, challenging me. "Go ahead. You know you want the satisfaction of seeing me canned. I can see it in your eyes. You hate me. Get your revenge."

I didn't hate him. This would be *so* much easier if I did.

I swallowed past the words dying to come out. The ones that begged him to not really be a spy or a traitor. The ones that would kill my pride with one great, sweeping blow. I should do exactly what he said—call Dad. But if I did that, Dad would simply send another spy in. At least with Finn, I knew what to expect.

Was that reason enough to keep him around? I couldn't imagine having to see him every day after this. To be reminded of how much an idiot I had been, time and time again. "What will happen to your dad?"

Finn's façade crumbled. Guilt took its place, and he yanked on his hair. "He'll lose his big pension, but that's my responsibility to bear, not yours. Do it."

I liked his dad, but that wasn't why I hesitated. That wasn't why I wasn't pulling the trigger, so to speak. No, something besides empathy drove me. Something uglier and more self-serving. "You want me to do it. You want to be sent away, don't you?"

He held his hands out to his sides. "I don't know what you're insinuating."

"Ah, but I think you do." I pointed the phone at him, laughing lightly. "Is the guilt too much for you? Can't stand seeing the effects of your lies? Ready to run?"

"Yes, it's too much," he cried. "I hurt you and I'm *sorry*. I know you hate me, and I know why, but just fucking end it already, or I will."

I shook my head. "No, you're going to stay. You're going to watch me forget all about you. Watch me move on. You're going to do your duty, and you're going to report back to him like the good little spy you are."

He gave a harsh laugh. "Why the hell would I do that?'

"To save your father." I tilted up my chin. "And because you owe me. You made me want to be with you, then you turned out to be nothing but a fraud."

His face crumpled and he sank down on the couch. He looked as if he gave up. Stopped caring or hoping. "Fine. I'll do it."

"Good."

"I really am sorry," he rasped, his head low. I couldn't see his face, but the sincerity in his voice almost broke me. "I hope you know that."

I tensed, my whole body aching to go to him. To comfort him, of all things. I was really messed up in the head from all this crap. "The only thing I know now is what my father's spy looks like, and I want to *keep* knowing. You'll do your duty, but you'll stay the hell away from me. I don't want to see you, smell you, or even hear you. Just report back to my dad while leaving me the hell out of it."

He lifted his head, and the vulnerability I'd caught a glimpse of was gone. "I can't follow you around, watching you flirt with other men. Not anymore."

"You should have thought of that before we did what we did." I collected my books and lifted my phone to my ear. "Yes, I'd like a cab, please." I told the operator my location and hung up. "Text him and tell him I studied and went to bed early."

Finn picked up his phone and quickly typed. Then he threw it down on the couch. "You have no idea what you're starting here. You should report me immediately."

"I should, but I won't." I looked out the window, waiting for the cab.

"Why not?"

I forced a shrug. "Because I want to know what to expect. Because I'm more like my father than I realized. I like being in control too."

"With me, you've never been in control."

"Yeah, I know that now." I blinked back tears, refusing to show him how much I hurt. Refusing to show him my weakness—him. "But from now on, I will be."

I hurriedly gathered the rest of my things, including my shirt I couldn't find earlier, and he stayed quiet. Thank God. I couldn't pretend like I wasn't dying inside any longer. Couldn't pretend he hadn't broken my heart, when he had. If he knew how hard I had fallen, he would never leave me alone. Never let me move on. And I *needed* to move on.

The cab beeped from outside, and I turned to face him. He watched me with a weird mixture of apprehension and longing. "I don't want to see you watching me. Just do your job, and stay out of my way."

When I headed for the door, he stood up. "I'm sorry, Gi—" He broke off. "Carrie. I really am."

I paused with my hand on the knob, squeezing it so tightly my knuckles hurt. "So am I."

I opened the door and walked out of his apartment for the last time. I had no intention of ever stepping foot inside it again. I didn't want to see him again either. Didn't need the reminder that he had stolen my heart and then stomped it into the dirt.

If only he had buried it too.

CHAPTER NINETEEN

Finn

A few days later, and a hell of a lot of thinking and heartache later, I grabbed my phone, jotted off a quick text to Senator Asshole letting him know his daughter was still alive, and then grabbed my surfboard. It had been too long since I'd been out in the ocean alone. Too long, especially since it was pretty much the only place that no one bugged me or talked to me or told me to fuck off.

The past few times I'd come had been with Carrie, but those days were obviously over. Shit, we *were* over, and I was miserable because of it. I missed her. Missed having her in my arms. Missed the man I was with her. She made me better. Different. Whole.

But not anymore. I was destined to walk around half-filled for the rest of my miserable life. With a sigh, I juggled my board and closed the door, making sure to lock it, then headed for my bike. After sliding my surfboard into the special slot I'd had added on to the side earlier this week, I revved the engine and pulled away from the curb. The wind blew through my hair since I hadn't grabbed my helmet, and I took a deep breath.

I hadn't expected to miss her so damn much once she left me. It had been a relationship born out of lies and pretenses, but now I couldn't stop thinking about her. And she probably hadn't even thought of me once since the other day, besides to curse me out.

In all three languages she spoke.

She'd told me she could speak three languages. I also knew she let out a tiny little snore every once in a while when she slept. She gave almost all of her allowance to the poor and rarely spent any money. She liked her milkshakes creamy, not watery. I hadn't read any of that in her file. There was so much I knew about her that her damn file didn't know. We had surpassed the working relationship I'd meant to maintain a long time ago. But to her, that's all I'd ever be.

The guy who was sent to spy on her by her daddy.

Ever since she told me to leave her alone, she'd spent almost every passing second with Cory. They ate together. Walked together. Studied together. They seemed to be attached at the hip, and it was driving me insane with jealousy each time I saw them. Ripping my chest open until a tiny little monster grew bigger than fucking Godzilla. A part of me was sure she was hanging with that loser just to hurt me.

But she didn't believe me about how much I cared for her—refused to believe me. So she wouldn't be trying to hurt me if she thought I was just talking to her for the job, which only made it worse. It meant that every time she laughed at something Cory said and hugged the jerk closer, it was *real*. It wasn't some scheme to torture me.

She actually liked the little fucker.

I parked my bike and slid off the seat. After taking off my shirt, I put on my wetsuit, my eyes on the blue water. It looked particularly impetuous today. Good. I was in the mood to get tossed around. Hard. I headed for the beach, excitement taking over for the first time since Carrie had broken it off with me. I would get out there, ride a few waves, and forget all about—

"Why are *you* here?" Carrie asked from somewhere behind me.

I paused midstride, my heart leaping at the sound of her voice. God, I had missed hearing that sass in her tone. That spark of something that no one else could possibly bring out in me. I forced a neutral expression to my face and turned to face her.

She wore her wetsuit, but had it down around her waist, and her unruly hair was pulled back in a ponytail. She had big bags under her eyes, as if she'd been sleeping poorly. I forced my attention to return to the ocean, and said, "I'm going to church."

"Haha." Out of my peripheral vision, I saw her eye my surfboard, her blue eyes cold and her lips pressed tightly together. Her small spattering of freckles danced across her nose, and her curly red hair already whipped across her forehead. She looked perfect. "Very funny, but don't quit your day job of stalking college girls."

"It wasn't supposed to be funny or a joke. This *is* my version of church." I felt stupid for letting her know how I really felt about surfing, but there was no going back now. I'd already opened my big fat mouth. I shrugged and tried my best to look like I didn't give a damn what she thought about me. "When I'm out there, it's just me, God, and the ocean. No one else can interfere with me except Mother Nature herself."

She nibbled on her lower lip. "That's awfully profound for a surfer boy."

"I'm more than just a surfer boy, but you already knew that, didn't you?"

She crossed her arms. "I'm going surfing today, so you can't go."

"Excuse me?" I laughed at her audacity. "I hate to break it to you, but you don't own the ocean, Princess."

She stiffened. "No, but you work for my family and I don't want you out there with me, so you have to listen to me. I'm your boss."

Okay, that stung a little bit. It would be a lie to say it hadn't. "The hell you are. I work for your father."

Her face turned red. "Just go away. I don't want to be out there with you."

"Then surf farther south. Or north, for all I care." I gestured toward the ocean with my board. "This is my beach, and I'm not leaving it. Not even for you."

"I thought no one owned the beach," she called out, taunting me. Even her stance was aggressive, her feet spread wide and her eyes flashing with anger. She wanted a fight, and she wanted it bad.

I wouldn't rise to the bait. Wouldn't fight. But I sure as hell wouldn't back down either. "They don't, but this is the beach my mother took me to every weekend as I grew up. It's where we had our last night together, before she was gone forever. And it's the beach I rode my first wave on, with her by my side. I'm sure as hell not leaving it because you hate me."

I brushed past her, fully intending to leave her standing on that beach alone, but her soft word stopped me. "Wait."

"What now?" I asked, my entire body tense.

"I'm sorry. You're right." I turned to face her, and she swept her hair out of her face with a frustrated sigh. "I'm being a bitch. Just because I can't stand the sight of you doesn't mean I get to tell you to leave."

"Such a heartfelt apology."

She lifted a shoulder. "It's the best I can do, considering."

"May I go now, *boss lady*?" I cocked my head toward the ocean. "I'd like to enjoy the type of solitude only the ocean can give me before it's too late."

"You never mentioned wanting solitude out there before."

"That's because I was with you," I reminded her.

She cocked her head. "Why did you take me, if you didn't like going out there with other people?"

"Because with you? I didn't mind."

I headed for the ocean once more, leaving her standing there. She wouldn't believe me anyway, so there was no point in waiting to see if she replied. She'd just accuse me of running a play on her, or trying to win her over so I could babysit her better. I wasn't in the mood to get my heart trampled again.

Just my body.

I almost made it to the water before I got interrupted again. I bit back a curse when a blonde in a skimpy bikini stopped me. "Hey. Remember me?"

I scanned her face. Nope. I didn't. "Uh...?"

"I work at Surf's Up," she said, punching my arm lightly. "I helped you pick out your girlfriend's surfboard."

"She's not my girlfriend," I said, my eyes automatically scanning the beach for Carrie. She stood a few yards away, her own gaze on me...and the blonde at my side. "We're not even friends anymore, really."

Her nostrils flared. Could she hear us? She looked ready to kill someone. I wasn't sure if her target was the girl or me—maybe both.

"Oh, well, I like the sound of that." She trailed her fingers over my tattoo, giving me a flirtatious smile. "I like your ink. What's it mean?"

I hated when girls asked that. It wasn't any of their damn business what my ink meant. "Thanks, and nothing. It's just ink."

"Oh. Hot."

That was...deep. About as deep as a puddle. I cleared my throat and looked at Carrie again. Her fists were clenched at her sides. Was she jealous? Nah. Not possible. "You surf?"

The blonde laughed and punched me again. Why did girls think that was sexy? I only liked one girl hitting me, but she didn't even want to touch me right now. Or ever. "No, I just help out at the store, and I date a lot of surfers. *Only* surfers."

Before I could reply, Carrie walked up to some shirtless guy. She smiled at him and handed him sunscreen. The jerk smiled back at her and Carrie turned her back to the guy. When the jerk squirted sunscreen on his hands and massaged it over Carrie's shoulders, I clenched my teeth. Carrie laughed at something the guy said, slapping his arm lightly. The jerk didn't seem to mind either.

"You've got to be kidding me," I murmured. "I'm going to kill her."

Blondie shot me the dirtiest look ever. "Just friends, huh?" Then she was gone.

I stood there, trying to figure out what the hell had just happened.

Carrie. That's what happened.

She thanked the helpful guy, then headed for the water, pulling up her wetsuit. I caught up to her within seconds. "What was that all about?"

"What?" She blinked at me innocently, but the smirk was harder to hide. "I needed sunscreen."

"Under your wetsuit?"

"Sure. You can never be too careful." She shrugged. "Did you have fun with Bambi over there?"

And just like that, I relaxed. "You're jealous."

She snorted and snorted again. As if such a preposterous statement required a double snort. "I am *not.*"

"Oh. So, if I go out there and flirt with her, you won't give a damn?"

"Good luck with that. She probably hates you now." Carrie splashed into the water, sending droplets my way. "As a matter of fact, I might have to watch you get rejected. It'll be funny and good for your ego."

I stared at her. "Is that a challenge?"

"No." She eyed me. "Knowing you, she'd be in your bed by nighttime. You'd like that, wouldn't you?"

I tensed. She made me sound like a manwhore, and I wasn't. I wasn't a virgin, but I didn't sleep around either. "Because I've given you reason to believe I'm a manwhore?"

"Stop asking me rhetorical questions."

I gripped my board tighter than I should have, but I couldn't help it. I wanted to scream. "That wasn't rhetorical. I'd *love* to know why you think I'd bring her home with me mere days after we broke up."

"You brought me home."

I rolled my eyes and fought against the huge wave trying to knock me down. "Oh, well, then I must be a whore. If I'll bring you home, anyone will do."

She whirled on me. "Yeah, pretty much."

"Wave."

"*What?*"

A wave knocked into her, throwing her in my arms. I caught her, stumbling back a bit before I caught my own balance again. As soon as I gained my footing, she quickly shoved out of my arms. "Wave," I repeated.

"I noticed." She shoved her damp hair out of her face. "Thanks for the warning."

I couldn't tell if she was being sarcastic, so I nodded. "Might want to face outward from now on."

"Gee, thanks for the pro tip." Another wave crashed into us, and she stumbled back. I started to reach for her elbow, but she shot me a supersonic death glare. "I'm fine. Stop protecting me."

"It's my job. Don't want my help? Go over there." I pointed to a crowded spot in the ocean. "They won't give a damn if you wipe out."

She lifted her chin. "I'm staying here."

"Thought you didn't want to be near me."

Did her chin go even higher? Yep. It did. "I don't, but I refuse to run away just because you're here."

"Lucky me," I drawled.

Another big wave came, and she stumbled backward again. I swallowed the sense of premonition creeping up. The ocean was perfect for me today, but for a novice like Carrie, it could be a deathtrap. If she got taken under by a monster wave, I might not be able to reach her in time.

She glanced at me out of the corner of her eye. "Why do you look like someone might take away your favorite toy?"

I shook my head. "I was quiet. That's all." Another wave came, and

I made a big show of getting knocked back. "Wow, the waves are pretty rough. Maybe we shouldn't surf today."

She eyed all the other surfers, who were smiling and laughing and catching waves. They weren't exactly helping my cause. "They all look fine to me."

"They're idiots for being out here in this. I don't know what I was thinking." I grabbed her elbow. "Let's go back to the shore."

She jerked free. "No."

"Carrie—"

"*No.*" She kept going farther into the ocean. I could tell by the way she stomped through the water that I wouldn't win this one. "Now go away. You've got an appointment with Jesus, and he doesn't like to be kept waiting."

I squared my jaw. "It's too dangerous for a newbie like you."

"For your charge, you mean?" She glanced back at me over her shoulder. "Oh well. You'll be earning your keep today, *guard.*"

Fine. She wanted to be like that? She could be like that. I followed her, muttering under my breath, "After you, *boss.*"

Looked as if my day of planned solitude was off. I wouldn't get the brief time of no one bossing me around or bugging me. Instead, I'd have to save her life time and time again. If she went and tried to drown on me, I'd rescue her and then throttle her little ass for being so damn reckless.

CHAPTER TWENTY

Carrie

Once I got out into the ocean, I straddled my board, determined not to let Mr. Worrywart take the fun out of my morning. It had been a long, painful week and I needed to let go. Needed to relax. But then he came. I knew there was an easy fix to this annoyance. Knew I could swim away from him, and our entire interaction would be over. But if I did that, he might start flirting with Bimbo Bambi again. And for some reason I didn't want to name right now, thank you very much, I didn't want him talking to her.

Or looking at her.

Or thinking about her.

No big deal, right? Right.

He paddled closer to me and gave me a long, hard look. "So, where's Lover Boy today?"

Lover Boy? As if. "Don't you call him Golden Boy?"

"Yeah, I did, but I changed my mind lately. Where is he?"

"He's not the surfing type," I said simply.

The truth was, I hadn't invited him. Why would I? This wasn't his thing. It was mine. Besides, I had been spending way too much freaking time in his company lately. He was a perfect gentleman. He didn't do a single thing wrong. Never lost his temper or fought with me. Never called me annoying nicknames. He treated me like a princess.

Turns out, I didn't like being treated like a princess.

I liked annoying surfer boys who lied to me.

"No kidding," he said dryly. "I never would've guessed that."

"Talk to Jesus, not me."

"I can't. I only talk to him when I'm alone."

I saw a wave coming in the distance, but quickly realized it would be too big. I knew not to ride the huge ones. Knew I was a novice at best. He worried for nothing. Small correction—he worried about me because he was *paid* to do so.

"You get this one."

He hesitated. "You going to be okay alone?"

"Yes, yes." I rolled my hand in a sweeping gesture. "Just *go*."

He gave me one last look before paddling forward. Despite my annoyance with him, I couldn't help but watch in admiration. He sliced through the wave as if he was born on a surfboard, and he made it look damned sexy. Effortless too. I could sit here all morning, watching him surf.

Talking to him. Fighting with him. Kissing him...

God, what was wrong with me? Why was I still thinking about him like this after what I'd found out? After knowing he'd been paid to get close to me? To fool me into liking him. I was sick. I would never have believed myself possible of such weakness before Finn.

By the time he made his way back, I was thoroughly disgusted with myself. He grinned at me and shook his head like the dog he was. Droplets landed on my nose, and I swiped them off. "That was a great one."

I clucked my tongue and kept staring straight ahead. Not looking at him. "I saw."

"You okay?" he asked after a moment's hesitation.

"I'm freaking wonderful."

I checked over my shoulder, but it didn't look like any waves of an appropriate size would be coming anytime soon. Maybe he'd been right, and I should've left, but then I'd have to admit defeat to him...and I wasn't willing to do that. Not ever again, if I could help it.

He looked out at the ocean too, his brow furrowed. "We could just head in. You can try tomorrow."

"Not happening. I'm riding at least one wave before I go home."

"You don't have to prove anything to me," he said, his voice low. "We both know you're good at surfing, but that's exactly why you can't take one of these. You know you're not ready."

"Don't tell me what I can and can't do," I said, my grip on my board tight. "I'll take whatever wave I want, whenever I want it, and you can't do a darn thing to stop me."

"The hell I can't," he snapped, throwing his left leg over the side of his board. "Watch me."

"Stop right there," I warned, holding my hand out. If he touched me, I would be done for. I couldn't ever feel his touch again, because if I did, I might just forget all about the lies. I might not care anymore. "I'm warning you."

"Or what? You'll yell at me some more?"

He hopped off his board and started swimming to me. Oh God. I had to get away. Needed to escape. He'd triggered the fight-or-flight response in my system, and I chose flight. I glanced behind me just in time to see a wave forming. It was bigger than usual, but nothing too insane.

He must've seen the look in my eyes, because his own went wide. "Don't do it, Carrie. You can't—"

"The hell I can't," I echoed back at him, paddling forward.

"Carrie, no!" he yelled. He leapt on his board, clearly trying to catch the wave with me.

I had no idea if he succeeded, because I was trying to keep my balance since the "not so big wave" turned out to be *humongous*. I was an idiot for trying to ride it. Within seconds, I wiped out, the salt water stinging my eyes and filling my mouth. I hadn't held my breath. Hadn't been ready. I'd been too busy worrying about him and what he was doing.

I went under hard, and my tethered surfboard hit me in the back of the head. Stars swam before my eyes, but I tried to wait out the torrential wave like Finn had taught me. I got thrown around like a limp rag doll in a washing machine. Oh, God, I was going to die out here in the cold Pacific Ocean, all because I'd been too much of a fool to know when to call it quits. Too darn full of pride for my own good.

What would happen to Finn when he realized I wasn't coming back up? How could it be that we would never see each other again? There was so much more to talk about. Things to figure out and fights to have. I wasn't ready to die yet.

A hand closed around my wrist, yanking me up to the surface. Before I could so much as blink in surprise, my face cleared the water. Finn took a deep gulping breath, then disappeared below the ocean.

"Finn!" I screamed, paddling around in a frantic circle. "*Finn!*"

Nothing. He was gone.

I took a deep breath and sank under water, but I only just got my head under when someone from behind me yanked me back up. I let out a broken sob and broke free. "No! He's missing!"

I dove back under the water, but my captor caught my arm again. I swung a fist at him, refusing to be held back when Finn needed help. Refusing to let him die because he'd saved me.

"Jesus, Ginger," Finn said, shaking me. "I'm right here." He shook me again. "Carrie, I'm here."

I stopped fighting and took a deep, ragged breath. He was here. Alive. I burst into tears and threw my arms around his neck. He hugged me tight and kissed my temple, then my cheek. I held my breath, waiting to see if he'd take it further. If he'd kiss me. He seemed to hesitate, his lips hovering near mine. So close I could move just a tiny bit, and we would be touching.

But I held my breath for nothing, because he didn't move that inch, and neither did I. "Sh. It's okay. You're okay. I got you."

I choked on a sob and hit his shoulder. "I wasn't worried about *me*, you idiot."

"Well, you should have been." The calming tone he'd been using disappeared and was replaced by the hard, cold tone he'd never used on me before. "Fuck, Carrie. You could've died. All because of what?"

"Because of you!" I hit him again, but he didn't even flinch. "Because you won't leave me alone! I had to get away."

He flinched. "Well, from now on, I will. Believe me, I will," he rasped, his voice breaking on the last word.

He started for the sand. Part of me wanted to continue this fight out here in the ocean, but the other part of me wanted to get him safely to the shore. I had almost *lost* him. Really lost him. When he'd sunk under the water, I had gone insane with worry. And the way I felt at the mere idea of losing him told me something I should have known already.

I wasn't over him. I might never be completely over him.

As soon as my feet cleared the hectic rush of the water, he let go of me and dragged his hands down his face. "Jesus."

"What did you mean out there?" I asked, unable to stop myself. "About leaving me alone?"

He turned to me, his face drawn and ragged looking. "I didn't know you hated me so much you'd rather die than surf next to me."

I swallowed hard. That wasn't it at all. I didn't hate him. That was the problem. "I can't surf with you or be your friend. I don't even want to see you. It hurts too much."

He paled. "It hurts me too. You have no idea how damn much it hurts because you think this was all a game to me. It wasn't. And seeing you every day? It *kills* me."

I pressed a hand to my heart, the pain he'd sent slicing through it with his words was almost knee buckling. Okay. So maybe he really had cared about me, at one point. But it didn't change the fact that he'd lied to me. Or the fact that he'd been spying on me for money. For my father. I cared about him too, but nothing could change any of those things… no matter how much I wished it could.

Because I really did.

"Then it's settled." My throat was so swollen with pending tears that I could barely speak, let alone breathe. "It's better if we avoid places we used to hang out. You watch me from a distance as you have been this week, and we don't come out here anymore. Don't see each other."

He cleared his throat. "You won't see me again. Goodbye."

Wait. I couldn't do this. Couldn't let him walk away from me. There had to be a way to at least be friends. Or to try. "Finn, I—"

"Don't. Just don't." He shrugged. Actually shrugged, as if he didn't care at all. "It doesn't even matter, does it? We didn't ever stand a chance."

My throat ached from the tears I held back. The tears I wasn't sure I could hold back anymore all because I'd gone and fallen for my bodyguard. "Not with all the lies."

"Right." He laughed. "It was all a mistake. One huge fucking mistake, but it's easy to fix. As easy as walking away." He gave me one last long, hard look, then said, "Goodbye, Carrie."

"Finn…" I held my hand out, but he'd already turned his back on me.

He walked away, his back stiff and his head held high. The tone in his voice was so…so final. As if he meant what he said, unlike me. And I had a feeling he would be better at sticking to his word than I was too.

I wouldn't see him again.

CHAPTER TWENTY-ONE

Finn

Three agonizing weeks later, I sat on a bench, an open technology textbook perched on my knee and a hat pulled low over my head. All part of my incognito spy outfit. That way if she saw me, I wouldn't be instantly recognizable. It had worked so far. We hadn't spoken since that day in the water, and she hadn't looked at me even once.

I'd seen to it.

It was five o'clock, and the soft ocean breeze calmed my otherwise fraught nerves. Soon she would come out. I'd been following her around. Watched her help out at the cancer race. Watched her go to the soup kitchen, even though I stood outside of it now. Watched her give away clothes and food and money—but not once had she done anything fun for herself. She just studied and helped and volunteered.

No fun. No games. Hardly ever any smiles.

If I didn't know better, I'd think she missed me. But she didn't.

Carrie came out of the building five minutes earlier than usual, her hair frizzy and her face lowered. Even with her hair sticking up every which way to Sunday, she was the picture of perfection. A breath of fresh air on a hot, smoggy day. I tensed as she walked right past me, but she didn't even glance my way.

She pressed a hand to her stomach, her steps quickening. Was that a groan I heard? No, I must've been imagining things. I stood up, tucking the book into my bag as I shadowed her steps. She walked faster than usual, but had some odd kind of shuffle to her step. Like a supersonic zombie. What was wrong with her?

When she slapped a hand over her mouth and ran for the cover of the bushes that lined either side of the walkway, I got my answer. She was sick. I sprinted after her, my stomach twisting in response to the retching sounds that came from her. Any time someone vomited, I always felt sympathy nausea. Sometimes, that sympathy turned into my own bout of puking my guts up.

So, as a rule, I avoided people who were throwing up, but this was *Carrie*.

I dropped to my knees at her side, grabbing her hair and holding it back from her face so she wouldn't get it dirty. She didn't even bother to look my way or tell me to fuck off. She just kept puking. A cold sweat broke out on my forehead, but I tightened my grip on her hair and made sure to breathe through my mouth—not my nose.

Shallow, slow breaths.

"Sh. It's okay." With my free hand, I rubbed her back in wide, sweeping circles. "I've got you."

She shuddered, one last gag making its way out of her body before she let her head hang. Not knowing what else to do, I kept rubbing her back and holding her hair. After what seemed like an eternity of sitting by the putrid vomit, she lifted her head. Her blue eyes were hard, but they held a touch of vulnerability to them.

"Go away, Finn," she mumbled. Swiping a hand across her mouth, she struggled to stand up. "I'm fine."

I quickly rose and lifted her to her feet. When she stumbled sideways, almost right into her puke, I gripped her hips. "Shit. Stay still."

"I'm trying," she muttered, clinging to my shoulders. "The world won't stop spinning."

"Can you walk?"

She lifted her chin. "Of course I can."

"Okay."

I let go of her, even though every instinct screamed at me to hold on tighter and never let go. She took one step and almost fell flat on her face. I caught her effortlessly, swinging her up in my arms.

Her head flopped down on my chest, and she looked anything but ready to be released. "God, it hurts."

"I'll take care of you."

"I can take care of myself," she mumbled, her eyes drifting shut.

My heart seized at the look on her face as she drifted off. She was pale and listless. Her small hand rested on my chest, right above my heart. She liked putting it there, as if she knew she owned it and was re-staking her claim. "I know you can, but I want to help you. Now rest."

I dropped a quick kiss to her clammy forehead and headed for my bike. I almost reached it before I realized I couldn't ride home with an unconscious Carrie on my lap. I hesitated, not sure what to do. Should I get a cab and take her back to my place? Or should I carry her up to her room and take care of her there?

I spotted Marie walking to the dorm, three girls on either side of her. They were laughing loudly, talking about a study session involving alcohol in Marie's room. Carrie stirred at their laughter, her brow furrowing. I held her closer, kissing her temple.

"Take me home," she muttered restlessly. She burrowed closer to me, let out a ragged sigh, and fell asleep.

Well, that settled it. Home. *My* home.

Walking right past my bike, I managed to call a taxi without waking Carrie. Once it arrived, I settled into the back of the cab with her curled up on my lap. I smoothed her hair off her face, studying her delicate features. Her small nose was red at the tip, and she had bags under her eyes that hinted she hadn't been sleeping well lately. I hadn't been either.

I missed Carrie too much.

Somehow I doubted I was the cause of her insomnia, though. More likely, it had been because she'd been hitting the books harder than usual. Midterms were coming up, so she had been preparing for those. I had seen her in the library with Lover Boy almost every day this week. Whenever she studied, Cory did too.

Fucking annoying pansy.

The cab stopped in front of my place, and I shuffled Carrie in my arms so I could reach my wallet. The cabbie eyed Carrie. "Is she dead? If so, it'll cost extra."

I rolled my eyes. "Glad to know humanity is still at its peak."

"Hey, I'm just sayin'."

"So am I." I tossed the cash at the man. "She's not dead. She's sick."

"Then get her out of my cab before she ruins it."

I glanced pointedly at the cigarette burns covering the seat and the crack in the glass of the window. "I think it's too late for that."

"Whatever." The man dismissed me with a casual flick of his wrist. "Just go."

I was getting damned sick of people telling me to "just go," but now wasn't the time to address that. I had a sick Carrie on my hands—one who might explode at any given time. I opened the door, hugging her closer to my chest as I bent to get out. She jerked awake, her eyes wide. She looked…ah, fuck.

She looked green.

I picked up the pace. "Are you going to make it inside?"

She nodded frantically and squeezed her eyes shut. I practically ran to my door, unlocked it, and deposited her in front of the toilet. She waved her hand at me, clearly wanting me to leave, but I hovered in the doorway. Though my stomach demanded I do as she wished, I couldn't *leave* her.

When the first tortured groan escaped her, I stopped trying to fight the inevitable. I kneeled beside her, grabbing her hair to keep it out of the path of destruction. Her body tensed, but she didn't have a chance to tell me to go away before the vomiting started again. My own stomach twisted in reply, but I gnashed my teeth. By the time she was finished, I knew I would be throwing up today too.

I stood, my legs shaking, and wet a washcloth with warm water. She rested her cheek on her forearm, which was flung over the side of the toilet. When I came back to her side, she opened her eyes and blinked at me, a tear rolling down her face. "This sucks," she whispered.

I dabbed the washcloth over her forehead and across her mouth. "I know."

"Why are you doing this?" She closed her eyes and took a deep breath. "It's not in your job description, is it?"

"Knock it the hell off." I flexed my jaw, tossing the washcloth in the corner of the bathroom. I picked her up. "I'm taking care of you, and you're not going to stop me."

She rested her head on my shoulder, her hand once again over my heart—which traitorously sped up. "I don't know why you could possibly want to."

"It should be obvious. If it's not, I'm not sure what to say." I lowered her to the bed and lifted the blankets until she was covered. "I'm going to go grab you some medicine. I'll be right back."

I headed for the bathroom and closed the door behind me. After turning on the shower, which I hoped would be loud enough to drown out the sound of what I was about to do, I fell to my knees in front of the porcelain god. I flushed the toilet, and within seconds my own stomach emptied itself.

By the time I was finished, I felt as shaky and weak as she'd looked. I flushed again, then hopped in the shower to make it look as if I'd showered instead of ralphed. I allowed myself a minute to quickly scrub down, brush my teeth, and throw a towel around my waist. Opening up the cabinet, I pulled out the Pepto-Bismol I'd bought a few weeks ago after I'd had some bad tuna.

I took a dose for myself behind the closed door, and then came out of the bathroom with hers. She was curled up on her side, her eyes open but sleepy. I sat down beside her and held out the medicine. "Here. Take this."

"Thank you." She sat up slowly, her gaze drifting over me. "Can you please lose the towel?"

I tensed. "Why?"

"Because I don't want to see you half naked." She licked her lips, her stare somewhere around the level of my abs. "Not anymore."

Liar. "Sure."

I stood up, dropping the towel to the floor. Her indrawn breath almost made me crack a smile, but I forced myself to remain dead serious. Hell, I even stretched my arms over my head, letting her look her fill for however long she'd like.

"Finn."

I looked over at her, butt-assed naked. "Yeah?"

"You're *naked*."

"I know." I looked down at myself. "You said to lose the towel. You also said you didn't want to see me half naked anymore, so here you go."

She set down her empty cup on the nightstand with a trembling hand, but her lips quirked as if a smile was trying to escape, but she didn't want to let it. I hadn't realized how much I missed her smile lighting up my life until now. "When I said 'lose the towel,' I meant put on some clothes. And by not wanting to see you half naked, I meant clothed."

"Oh." I shrugged. "I guess I could get dressed."

I crossed the room wearing my birthday suit, then opened my top drawer. She let out a strangled groan, but I heard her lay back down. Did she face the other way so she wouldn't have to see me anymore? Or was she watching? I dared a glance over my shoulder and quickly turned back around.

Oh, she was watching, all right.

I slowly stepped into a pair of boxers and pulled out a pair of khaki shorts. After I slid those on, I turned to face her. My stomach was a little bit steadier now. "Better?"

She cleared her throat. "Shirt?"

"Nah. I never wear one at home. You know that." I sat down beside her, reaching out to feel her forehead. It was blazing hot. "Shit, you have a fever."

She blinked at me. "Yeah, I've had one all day. Woke up with one."

"And you went to school *why*?"

She laid back down, cuddling into my bed as if she belonged there. And she did. She really fucking did. "I can't afford to miss classes right now."

"You can't afford to neglect your health either."

She rolled her eyes. Even sick and wasted, she had enough energy to give me sass and attitude. I loved it. Hell, I loved *her*, but that wasn't exactly a surprise to me. Not after all the moping I'd been doing ever since I lost her.

"My mom is all the way across the country and I'm single. Who am I supposed to get to take care of me?" she asked.

She didn't have to be single if she would give me another chance, but I didn't point that out. "Me."

"I can't call you for help anymore." She stared up at me. "We're not even really friends."

My heart wrenched, but I refused to show her how much it hurt for me to follow her rules. I pushed off the bed, heading into the kitchen. "I'll go make you some chicken broth."

"I'm not hungry." She rolled over and curled her knees into the fetal position. "Not even in the slightest."

I didn't stop walking. "You need something in your stomach, or it'll just hurt more when you puke."

"You don't have to do this," she called out, her voice shaking. "I'll be fine on my own."

"Yeah, I do. And no, you won't."

Because if I didn't take care of her…

Who would?

CHAPTER TWENTY-TWO

Carrie

I leaned back in the couch, holding the bowl in the crook of my lap. As I sipped down the chicken broth, I felt immensely better before it even hit my stomach. But even if it hadn't made me feel better, it was quite easily the most delicious soup I'd ever had. It didn't even have anything in it. Finn sat beside me on the couch, eating his own plain broth. He still hadn't put on a shirt, and I still hadn't stopped thinking about touching him again, even though I felt like I was on death's door.

I wouldn't follow through with my thoughts, but it didn't stop me from *wanting*.

He had a way of touching me that made me forget all about the outside world. All about how much he'd betrayed me, and how much I was supposed to hate him. I shouldn't be here, eating his soup and using his bed. I shouldn't be near him at all.

I still cared about him too much.

He looked at me out of the corner of his eye. "You okay?"

"Yeah." I set down my bowl. "That was really good. Thanks."

He finished his own bowl then set it next to mine. "It was my mom's recipe. My dad gave it to me when I was old enough to cook it myself. It always made me feel better when I was sick, so it seemed appropriate."

"Thank you," I said softly, oddly moved that he'd made me the same soup his mother made him. I wanted to hug him. To take away the brief shadows of grief I saw before he looked away.

He tugged at his brown hair. "Don't mention it. How about we get you back in bed now?"

I swallowed hard. Even the thought of crawling back into his bed sent shivers down my spine. The things we had done there… "I should go back to my dorm."

"Why bother? You won't get any sleep there with Marie. She has company." He pinned me down with his stare, his bright blue eyes on me. "I promise I won't touch you. You'll be perfectly safe here."

He didn't need to touch me to make me want him. That was the scary part. "Still."

"No." He stood, his jaw ticking. "I tried this the nice way, but I'll put it simply: You're not leaving. End of story."

Okay, that took away any lingering desire to kiss him. Then again, his arrogance usually did. "You don't own me. You're not my dad, and—"

"No, but I work for him, as you've reminded me every chance you get." He picked up his phone and waved it in front of my eyes. "And I'm not afraid to call him and get him down here. I'll tell him you're refusing medical treatment from the hospital."

I drew in a deep breath. "You wouldn't."

He raised a brow and started typing. I stood up and tried to snatch it out of his hands. My stomach protested the fast movement with a loud gurgle. "Stop it. Don't you *dare* call him."

"Then get in the fucking bed." He narrowed his eyes at me. "I can tell you're making yourself even sicker by arguing with me. Just lay down."

"I'm fine." My stomach twisted again, and I clutched it tight. Oh God, I was going to…

"Yeah. Sure you are," he drawled. He picked me up, and I closed my eyes as the room spun. I should point out I could walk on my own, but I didn't want to open my mouth right now. "Bathroom or bed?"

"Bathroom," I gasped, the vomit trying to escape even with the single word. "And leave me alone this time. I don't want you to see—" I broke off and covered my mouth.

He made it to the toilet in record time. "Not leaving."

I opened my mouth to argue, but the torrential vomiting pouring out of my system swallowed up the words. By the time I was finished, I felt more like the stuff floating in the toilet than a person. I hadn't even realized Finn held my hair until he released it, heading for the washcloths again.

Why was he being so…nice? So darn courteous and thoughtful and perfect? He needed to open his mouth and say something annoying really quickly before I fell for him all over again. He returned with a wet washcloth. He looked sweaty and a little pale himself. What was wrong with him?

"Here," he murmured, wiping my face down as he did last time.

I closed my eyes, tears threatening to escape me at his tender touch. "Why are you being so nice to me? And why are you shaking?"

"Because I care, even if it hurts." He tossed the washcloth aside and rose to his feet. "Do you want to shower?"

"Yes." I opened my eyes. He was leaning against the sink clutching his stomach. As soon as he saw I watched him, he straightened and headed for the faucet. "Are you okay?"

"I'm fine," he said dismissively. "Just worry about yourself."

I frowned. "Are you sick too?"

"No." The shower turned on, and he stuck his hand under the stream of water. Seemingly satisfied with the temperature, he went back to the sink and pulled out a light blue toothbrush. He opened the case and set it down on the sink. "Here. Use this."

I stood up and he grabbed my elbow. As if he was ready to catch me if I fell. But that was his job, wasn't it? I couldn't read anything more into it than that. "I don't have any clothes to change into."

He hesitated. "I don't want to leave you here alone to go get some."

"I'll be fine alone."

"I'm not leaving you."

I sighed, but inwardly I smiled. He seemed so worried about me, and it was hard not to be affected by his concern. No matter how stupid that made me. "I'll wear these again." I looked down at the dirty, wrinkled clothes. The ones that probably smelled worse than I did. "It's not a big deal."

"No, you won't." He let go of me. "I'll go get a T-shirt and a pair of boxers for you to wear. They'll be big, but it's better than what you've got on."

Wear his clothes? Somehow that didn't seem like a grand idea. His scent was already ingrained in my memory. Did I really need to wear it too? "But—"

"No buts." He headed for the door. "Just get in the shower. I'll push the clothes in through the door once you're in."

The door shut in my face, making me flinch. I took off my clothes and stepped into the water. Closing my eyes, I took a long breath. This is exactly what I'd needed—a fresh shower. A clean start. Hopefully the puking portion of my illness would be over now, and I could actually sleep.

I turned to search for the shampoo, but stopped mid-reach. Next to his manly shampoo he had apologized for last time I'd been here rested a fruity, girly shampoo and conditioner. When had he put that in there? Back when we were "dating"? Or was it for another girl? Even as I thought it, my heart screamed no. I didn't think he was seeing anyone else. He'd never given me a reason to believe he was. For all intents and purposes, the only woman he ever talked to was me. Just me.

But only because he has to, my inner voice so rudely reminded me.

I poured the shampoo into my palm, then scrubbed my scalp a bit harder than strictly necessary. Maybe that would make my smarter, annoying inner voice shut up. But instead, it simply reminded me of the last time I'd been in this shower. I hadn't been alone, and Finn had washed my hair far gentler than I was doing to myself. He'd been tender and loving and kind.

And then the next day, I'd found out who he was.

By the time I was out of the shower, I felt better physically, but much worse *emotionally*. After I dried off, I padded over barefoot to the toilet, where he'd apparently left a folded up T-shirt and a pair of boxers for me. I recognized the T-shirt. It was the red one I'd been wearing the day I found out who Finn really was.

I had washed it and set it on his porch step weeks ago.

Of course, that was after I'd slept with it on for a week. I hadn't wanted to give it back. It had smelled like him, even after a washing. He hadn't said anything to me about me bringing it back, but he hadn't had a chance to say anything at all until today. I hadn't even seen him in three weeks. Part of me had wondered if he'd quit and gone home.

That same annoying part of me was thrilled at being proved wrong.

I pulled the shirt over my head, inhaling deeply. Had he known giving me this shirt would affect me so deeply? Or had he just blindly reached in and grabbed the first thing he saw? Probably the latter. I picked up the toothbrush, did a quick cleaning, then steeled myself to face him again.

I opened the door and peeked out. He sat on the couch, texting someone. His girlfriend? My dad? The freaking Pope? Who knew. "Hey."

He clicked his screen off and stood up. He still didn't wear a shirt. Probably just to taunt me with the muscles I would never touch again. "You look like you feel better."

"I do." I crossed the room and climbed into the bed, tucking myself in. "Thank you."

He stood up and came to my side. Gently, he pressed his hand to my cheek. "You feel cooler too," he murmured, his blue eyes examining me.

Looking for signs of…what?

"Good."

"Yeah. Good," he said.

We fell awkwardly silent, neither one of us so much as moving. Daring to be the first to break the hold we had over one another. His phone buzzed, making me jump. He dropped his gaze and checked the message. I swallowed back the jealousy threatening to take hold. "Who are you talking to?"

"Hm?" He typed a quick reply. "No one."

"Is it her shampoo in there?"

That got his attention. He looked up at me, his brow furrowed. "Whose?"

"You tell me." I touched my damp hair. "There's girl shampoo in there. Are you seeing someone?"

"What? No." He shook his head, as if he couldn't believe I'd asked him that. "I got that for you, back when we were…well, you know."

"You did?"

"Yeah." He flushed and rubbed the back of his neck. "That's where the toothbrush came from too. After that first night, I went shopping while you were at school. I thought that maybe you were going to be spending a lot of time here, so I wanted you to have what you needed. But then…well, you found out who I was, and that was that."

"That was that," I repeated, thoroughly and utterly confused. Nothing about this man added up. He acted as if he really cared about me and wanted to be with me, but he worked for my *father*. And he was a liar. And manipulative. And bossy. And annoying.

And irresistible.

There were a million things I wanted to say, and at least a million reasons why I shouldn't say them. So I said nothing at all. When I remained silent, he shifted uneasily on the bed. "I'll sleep on the couch tonight. You can have the bed."

"Don't be ridiculous."

He arched a brow. "How am I being ridiculous?"

"You can sleep in the bed too." I flushed, searching for the right words to make it look like I offered because of practicality. I couldn't let him know how much I ached to sleep in his arms again. Or how horribly I'd been sleeping ever since we had broken up. Or how I missed him so much it *hurt*. "It's not like we've never, well, you know. Worse things have been done in this bed than sleeping together."

"Worse?"

"Crap." *Mental facepalm.* "Not that it was bad or anything—what we did. I mean, you know it wasn't."

His lips twitched. "Do I?"

I covered my face. "I'm done trying to talk."

He laughed and pulled my hands down. "Relax, you're fine."

"No. I'm not fine." I looked at him and his laughter faded away. "I'm not fine at all."

He swallowed hard. "Carrie..."

"Don't say it. Don't say anything." I rolled over on my side. "Just turn out the light. I'm tired."

After what felt like an hour, he finally turned off the light. I released the breath I'd been holding, willing my racing heart to calm down. As he lowered himself on the bed, keeping above the covers, he also let out a deep whoosh of air.

He remained blessedly silent. I didn't know if he went right to sleep, because as soon as I felt him next to me, I zonked out. When I woke up in the morning, he was gone. My clothes were washed and folded nicely at the bottom of the bed.

A note rested on top of it. I opened it with trepidation. What would he say? What could he say?

I'm sorry.

--Finn

That's it. Just three little words. And yet, they were more than enough.

CHAPTER TWENTY-THREE

Finn

Two days later, I leaned against the outside of Carrie's dorm, my eyes on the building she was currently in. I knew exactly who it belonged to, and I also knew how much I hated that she was inside of it. With the man she should have fallen for all along.

Fucking Lover Boy himself, in the flesh.

Ever since the night she'd spent at my apartment, I'd resumed following Carrie around sight unseen. Just like she wanted. Yesterday, she'd kept darting glances all around, watching for me. Almost as if she wanted to catch me out of place. I'd made sure to stay out of sight, and she had eventually stopped looking.

I didn't blame her in the least. If our roles were reversed, I would've felt the same way. I wouldn't want to ever see her again, but that didn't make it any easier on me. Losing her had only made it all the more evident that I loved her. And all the more evident that I was an idiot too. The two kind of went hand in hand, didn't they?

Love didn't come without a little bit of stupidity. Okay. A hell of a lot of it.

The door opened, and Cory came out, his arm thrown around Carrie's shoulders. I tensed. She didn't shrug free like she normally did. If anything, she snuggled in closer. I clamped my jaw tight and proceeded to try and come up with at least twenty different ways I could shove

Cory's arm up his own ass. I'd only reached option three when Cory kissed Carrie's cheek, then went back inside.

Cheek? Fucking pansy…

I'd never like that guy as much as I did right now.

Carrie hugged her books tight to her chest and searched the empty courtyard. I should slink back into the shadows. Hide. But I didn't want to. Maybe I was in the mood for a fight. Maybe I just wanted to hear her voice as she told me to go away. Either way, I was completely pathetic.

I straightened, waiting to see if she would see me. Equally worried she might not. Her gaze skimmed over me, then slammed back. I stood my ground, waiting to see what she did. How she would react to my blatant disobedience to her request.

Mumbling to herself, she crossed the yard. "Hey. Thank you for taking care of me the other day."

She said it so fast that I had a hard time keeping up with the torrent of words coming out of her mouth. I cocked a brow. "You're welcome. Sorry I'm still here. I wasn't expecting you to come out of his room so soon." I shrugged and focused on the door behind her. "I figured you might be…ah, *busy* for a little while. Ya know."

Her cheeks turned pink. "We weren't…I didn't…" She pressed her lips together. "We were studying, not doing *that*."

Relief rushed through me, heady and unstoppable. Relief I didn't have a right to feel. "I figured as much when he kissed you on the cheek. Anyone who has earned the right to kiss you wouldn't go for your cheek."

She opened her mouth, then slammed it shut. "Good night, Finn. You can go now."

I cocked my head. "I'll leave once you're inside."

"I'm not going inside." She fluttered her hand. "Well, I am, but I'm coming back out. I'm going to a party."

I stood up straight at that. "What kind of party? And do you really think that's best after the way you felt a couple nights ago?"

"A frat party, and I'm fine."

She moved past me, going inside. I should go back into the shadows, but I didn't like the idea of her going to a party tonight. After the type of night she had the other day, she needed rest and tea. Not dancing and beer.

I paced for what had to have been twenty minutes, my impatience growing with each step I took. She had no place partying tonight. None at all. The door opened behind me and I spun. "You're not going to that party. If you think I'll sit there watching—"

I stopped talking, and my jaw dropped. Holy. Fucking. Shit.

I'd seen her in a bikini. I'd seen her surfing. I'd even seen her naked, but I had never seen her like *this*. She wore a tiny, poor excuse for a dress, a pair of *fuck me* heels that were meant to be over my shoulders, not on the ground—and wore more makeup than I'd ever seen on her before. Her red lips begged to be kissed, and the rest of her…well, it matched the shoes.

"*No.*" My jaw ticked. "Go upstairs and put on some real clothes."

She laughed. "Yeah, not happening."

"You're right. It's not." When she tried to pass me, I stepped in her way. "I said get dressed."

She shook her head. "No."

"Do it."

"Or what?" She put her hands on her hips. Actually put her hands on her hips and stared me down. "What can someone like *you* do to hurt me?"

I'd said almost those same exact words to her not long ago. Turns out, someone like her could hurt me too easily by refusing to be with me. By not loving me back. "I'll kiss you, like you did to teach me a lesson, if you don't change right now."

"Please." She huffed. "I'm not the one who can't handle a simple kiss."

Challenge. Accepted.

I hauled her close, making sure to press my body fully against hers. Closing my hands around her ass, I rubbed against her as I fused my mouth to hers, not wasting even a second in ravishing her. Her hands pushed at my shoulders, but then she stopped pushing and started pulling me closer. When her tongue dueled with mine, I barely managed to hold back my shout of satisfaction.

She might keep saying she didn't want to be around me, but her body obviously did. Thank fucking God. She whimpered into my mouth and lifted her leg, wrapping her calf around mine. I would like nothing more than to keep this going. To take her home with me and show her exactly how much she hated me while I made love to her repeatedly. But I knew as soon as the kiss ended, so would we.

Again.

I pulled back and rested my forehead on hers, wishing that things could be different. "I miss you," I whispered. "So damn much. Please give me another chance."

Her fingers tightened on me, and for a second I thought she might pull me closer. For a second, my heart leapt. She pushed me away. "I'm sorry, but I *can't*."

My heart leapt right into a gnarled mess at her words, but I forced myself to let her go. "Fine, but either you change out of that poor excuse for a dress, or I stay by your side all night instead of letting you do your thing undisturbed. Your choice."

"Why do you give a damn what I do? Just tell Dad I'm in bed. He won't know."

I shook my head. "I care because I care about you, Captain Obvious."

"Stop *saying* that."

"No." I advanced on her. "I care about you, and you telling me to stop isn't going to work. Get changed, or hang out with me."

"I'm this close," she held her fingers close together and shoved them in my face, "to calling my Dad and telling him I know exactly who you are."

I cocked a brow. "Go ahead."

Bluff. Called.

She stomped her foot. "What would your dad do without his pension?"

"If he was here, he'd be stopping you from leaving in that too." I dragged a hand through my hair. "This isn't you, Carrie. If you have to dress like this to get a guy's attention, he's not the right guy for you."

She held her hands out to her sides. "What would you know about what kind of guy I need?"

My jaw ticked. "I know it's not whoever you're wearing this outfit for."

"Oh?" She paced in front of me. "Let me guess. You're the type of guy I need?"

"No," I said honestly. "You deserve much better than me."

That made her stop pacing, and she looked at me in surprise. "Excuse me?"

"You heard me." I caught her jaw and tilted her face up to mine. "I'd like to say I deserve you, but the truth is I don't and never will. You deserve a prince, and you're not going to catch him wearing that."

"Finn…" She swayed toward me, her eyes soft. "I wish—"

"Is there a problem here?" Cory asked, his voice tight. He glared at my hand, which was still on Carrie's jaw. The little fucker was probably mad I dared to touch her. "Carrie? Are you all right?"

"I'm fine," Carrie quickly replied. "We were just finishing up here."

I dropped my hold on Carrie. "There's not a problem, Cody. Carrie was about to go change."

"Change?" Cory looked her up and down, and I swore the idiot's tongue hit the dirt. "She looks great to me."

"Of course she does," I muttered.

Carrie shot me an angry look. "Thank you, *Cory.*"

"This is touching and all," I said as I crossed my arms and rocked back on my heels. "but what's your choice?"

"I *choose* to ignore you and leave with Cory," she said, tipping her perfect little nose up in the air. "Now, if you'll excuse us?"

Cory threw an arm over Carrie's shoulder and shot me a triumphant grin. "See ya later."

I fell into step beside them. "No need for goodbyes. I'm coming along."

"No, you're not." Carrie stopped walking and shot me down with her sapphire eyes. "Finn. *Please.* Just go away. You're going to ruin everything."

She gave me the look she probably gave her father. The look that made her get away with everything in the world, and then some. The one that begged me to back off, before her cover was blown. If I kept insisting on accompanying her, questions would be asked. She would no longer be just another girl who went to college. She'd be the senator's daughter—complete with bodyguard.

"You heard her." Cory pulled Carrie closer to his side, eyeing me cautiously. "Go away. You don't even *go* to this school, do you?"

As if she needed protection from me. I was trying to help her, not hurt her.

Wasn't I?

Or was my jealousy the thing leading me to protest her outfit? Was it really any worse than what every other college girl would be wearing to the party? Maybe I needed to take a step back and stop playing the part of the overprotective boyfriend. I wasn't hers, and she wasn't mine. It was none of my business what she did or didn't wear anymore.

"Fine." I flexed my fingers. "You know where I'll be."

Carrie bit down on her lower lip and glanced away from me. "Thank you."

I inclined my head, shot a death glare in Cory's direction, and faded back into the shadows where I belonged.

CHAPTER TWENTY-FOUR

Carrie

Seeing Finn earlier had messed me up. Especially when he asked me to give him another chance. God, I wanted to, but I was too scared. Too scared to put myself out there again. Once a liar, always a liar. If he lied to me about his identity, what else would he lie to me about? What else had he *already* lied about?

I grabbed my fourth drink of the night, tipping it back and drinking deeply. It tasted like crap, but I didn't care. Not tonight. Seeing him had thrown me off-kilter. I'd been so sure I could get over him. Sure that eventually I wouldn't miss him or need him or want him. Then he'd had to go and kiss me. That had ruined everything. My body had responded immediately to him, as if it remembered the things he could do with his hands and tongue.

And it wanted more. *I* wanted more.

Marie came over to me, grinning. "Well, if it isn't the prodigal roommate. Out drinking like the rest of us college kids."

"Yeah." I forced a smile for my roommate. We weren't friends, but I didn't hate her. "Crazy, huh?"

"A welcome crazy." Marie nudged me with her shoulder. "I was starting to think I bunked with Mother Mary or something."

I rolled my eyes. "Believe me, that's not the case."

"Coulda fooled me." Marie took a long sip of her beer. "Although, I saw you on the beach the other week. Surfing. Who was that fine hottie you had with you? And more importantly, who is *he* to *you*?"

I tensed. "Him? No one. Nothing."

"Can you tell me where to find him? I'd like to be his something."

If Marie thought I would give her Finn's info, she was barking up the wrong tree. No one would be getting near him with my help while I still had breath in my lungs. "Sorry, I have no idea. He was just some guy..."

A soft laugh sounded from outside, and I glanced over my shoulder. Of course he'd heard that. I turned around and smiled at Marie. Luckily, she was too distracted to see the falseness behind the gesture. That, or she didn't care.

"Actually," I said, leaning closer. "I think he's gay."

"Really?" Marie gasped, her cheeks flushed. "Are you sure?"

I nodded, grinning when I heard a few mumbled curses from outside the open window. "Positive. He kept talking about Cory and asking if he was single."

Marie sighed. "It's true. All the good ones are gay or taken."

"Sadly so," I said, keeping my voice solemn, even though I wanted to cackle with glee. I pointed at a cute guy across the room, who was watching us. "But *he* looks single and straight."

Marie licked her lips. "Wish me luck."

"You don't need it," I said, smiling. "But good luck."

Marie took off, a swing in her step that hadn't been there a second before, and crossed the room to the guy. Within seconds of Marie leaving my side, Cory arrived. He threw an arm around me, throwing us both off balance. I didn't know how many drinks he'd had so far, but it had to be a lot.

Too many for him to be trustworthy.

Maybe he needed some fresh air to sober up. I fanned my cheeks again. "I'm hot. Can we go for a walk?"

Cory straightened and let out a hiccup. "Sure. Let's go."

He stumbled across the room, looking way too close to passing out, and I followed him. As soon as we stepped out into the night air, I took a deep breath. All of the colognes and booze had mixed into an unpleasant odor inside, and the fresh ocean breeze was a welcome change. I looked out toward the ocean and wrapped my arms around myself, reminded of another night just like this one.

The night I met Finn...

God, I missed him.

I gritted my teeth and turned to Cory, forcing a smile. I wasn't going to think about Finn anymore tonight. I refused. "It's been fun tonight."

"Yeah, I'm glad you came."

He wrapped his arms around me. It felt nice to be held by him. Secure, even. But I didn't itch to jump his bones. Didn't want to climb into his bed and lick him from head to toe. Maybe I was doing something wrong. Or maybe there was something wrong with me. Either way, I was done for the night. I wanted to go home.

I looked up at him, intending to tell him goodbye. I opened my mouth...and he was on me. His lips met mine, and it felt...nice. There might have been the slightest stirrings of desire, but it was so quiet a tiny breeze would have put out the fires. Cory groaned and crushed me against his chest, his tongue sliding in between my lips. I tried to feel something...*anything*...but it didn't work. There was nothing there, just like the other time he'd kissed me. Yeah, I was broken.

Why was it that only Finn could make me want him?

Just as I was about to pull back and make my excuses to go home, something crashed behind us. Cory jerked back from me and looked around. I, of course, knew who was out there. How could I have forgotten about Finn following me, for even a second? He'd seen us and probably thought I was moving on. I wasn't.

Probably never would be.

"Who's out there?" Cory asked, stalking toward the noise. "Show yourself."

I grabbed Cory's elbow, trying to bring him back. I didn't want them to see each other. "Don't worry about it. It was no one."

"Someone's watching you," Cory said, his jaw squared. "And I bet I know who it is."

"No!" I cried, trying to pull him back toward me. "There's no one out there. Let's go."

"I can *see* him." Cory pointed at where he supposedly saw Finn. "Come out here, surfer boy."

Finn stepped out of the shadows, his eyes hard and mouth pressed tight. His gaze skimmed over me, then slid back to Cory. "Don't call me that, Cody."

"I knew it was you. Why are you following her around?" He pushed Finn's shoulders and Finn stumbled backward. "Are you some kind of sicko who can't take no for an answer?"

Finn curled his hands into fists and stepped forward, his eyes narrow slits. "Push me again, and I'll be the sicko who breaks your fucking face."

Cory pushed him. Finn snarled and hauled back his fist, ready to do some damage. Cory, the fool, didn't even back off. He was either too drunk to see the immediate danger he was in, or he seriously underestimated Finn's strength. This wasn't going to end well.

I couldn't sit by and let Cory get hurt because I'd kissed him in front of Finn. Couldn't let *either* of them get hurt. I threw myself in front of Cory, arms akimbo. "Finn, *no*! Don't hurt him. I'm fine."

Finn's fist remained raised and something in his jaw ticked. "Get out of the way, Carrie."

Cory shoved me aside roughly, and I fumbled to regain my balance. "Yeah, let the freak stalker take his punch. I'll slam his white trash ass in jail so fast, he won't have time to say *lawyer up*."

"Stop being such a jerk, Cory. He's not a stalker," I said, tugging Cory back. My anonymity would have to come to an end. If I didn't tell Cory who Finn really was, he'd never shut up about this. Never back off. "He's my bod—"

"Ex-boyfriend," Finn interjected. "And I can't stop following her because I want her back."

I blinked at him. "We don't have to do this, Finn. Just tell him—"

"Good luck?" Finn slammed me with a look that clearly told me to play along. He didn't want me telling Cory who I really was. Why not? "I can't. I can't let another man have you."

Cory laughed. "Well, too late. She's already mine."

The hell I was. We would have a talk about Cory claiming me like that, but not now. Not in front of Finn. I shot a cautious look Finn's way. He still looked like he was ready to kill Cory, but at least he'd lowered his fist. "Let's go, Cory."

"Not until he tells me that he'll stop following you around all the time." Cory pulled free of my hold and stumbled back into the reach of Finn. "Did she tell you she wants to be with me instead? Are you mad she's mine instead of yours?"

Finn's fingers flexed. "Keep talking. Give me a reason to take a swing."

"It was only a matter of time until she came to her senses, you know." Cory smirked. "You might be fun for a while, but that's all you'll ever be to her—a fling."

I stiffened. I didn't like this side of Cory. Not one little bit. "Cory, stop it. You're being nasty. It's gross."

"Oh, *excuse* me. Should I bow at your feet?" Finn snorted. "Yeah. Keep dreaming, asshole."

"Go back to whatever trailer park you crawled out of, and leave us alone."

"*Cory.* Stop it!" I snapped. Finn's face revealed nothing, but I could feel how Cory's words affected him as if we were attached to one another. As if when Finn hurt, so did I. "Stop being this way. I don't like it."

"You'd best listen to her." Finn's nostrils flared and he advanced on Cory. "I suggest you leave before I forget that Carrie asked me not to kick your pasty white ass, *Cody.*"

Cory took a swing at Finn, connecting with his eye. Finn could've avoided it easily, I'd seen him do so. But he let Cory hit him. Why? Finn rubbed the spot where Cory had hit him, but not before I saw the blood and the bruise already forming. And then he grinned. *Grinned.*

"Game on," Finn said as he stalked toward Cory.

Cory paled, but stood his ground. He held up his fists. "Bring it."

That's it. I was leaving now, before I killed them both. Other girls might like being fought over, but I wasn't one of them. "Finn, *no.*"

Finn stopped midstride, his entire body humming with anger and something else I couldn't quite figure out. He took a step toward me and stopped. He tugged on the back of his head, torturing a poor curl. The look in his eyes haunted me. I'd hurt him. I could see it. Feel it.

"Leave. Now."

Cory smirked and walked right up to Finn. He leaned in and whispered something. Finn's face turned red, and then the next thing I knew, Cory was on the ground. He clutched his stomach, moaning and rolling around on the stone walkway. "You hit me. You actually *hit* me."

Finn dropped to his knees and hauled Cory up by the shirt, his face inches away from Cory's. "You ever say anything like that again, I'll fucking kill you. You hear me?"

Cory pressed his hand to his stomach. "I'm going to report you to the police."

Finn grinned, his eyes glinting maliciously. "Go ahead. Tell them I said hi." He dropped Cory back to the ground. "Now get the fuck out of here before I change my mind and kick your ass."

Cory stumbled to his feet and ran off, not even looking at me. His next stop would probably be reporting Finn to the police, and there would be repercussions from tonight. I closed my eyes and counted to three. "He's going to call the cops, and you're going to get arrested."

"Fuck him," Finn said, his voice tight.

I turned around to face Finn, but he had his back to me and his hands braced against a tree. "Did you *hear* me?"

His breath came fast and shallow. "I don't give a flying fuck what the hell he does."

"Well, I do." I grabbed Finn's shoulder and yanked. "What the hell is wrong with you?"

He spun on me, his entire body trembling with rage. "What's wrong with me? Do you actually have to ask me that?"

"Yeah, I do!" I grabbed his arms and shook him. "You aren't allowed to fly off the handle like that. You aren't allowed to draw attention to yourself. You *know* that. What will my father say about this? What about your dad?"

He flung me off him. "I don't give a damn anymore. Not about you. Not about anything."

I stumbled back from the force of his words. It would've been kinder if he had hit me. "You know what? Go to hell."

"Too late. I'm already there."

"You have no idea what hell is. Hell is falling for someone for the first time and finding out that everything he ever told you was a lie. That everything you wanted to believe in was all a ruse to get close to you."

He swallowed hard and closed his eyes. His hands fell at his sides, limp. "I didn't lie to you about us. I've already told you that a million times, didn't I?"

I shoved his shoulders, choking on the huge lump in my throat. Tears filled my eyes, but I blinked them back. I didn't have time for tears right now. "You're not allowed to be hurt in this situation. *You* were the one who did this. *You* were the one who went and ruined everything."

"You think I don't regret it? Huh?" He ran his hands down his face and let out a strangled growl. "You think I don't wish I could make it all go away, if only for one more night in your arms?"

I wanted that too. Only I wanted more than a night. I wanted to go back to what we'd been to each other. No lies. No secrets. "Well, we can't have that, can we?"

He dropped his hands to his side. "And I can't sit here watching you fall in love with someone else. Especially him."

"I'm not falling in *love* with him," I said, my voice coming out thick. No, I was in love with Finn and had been since the second he walked into my life. There wasn't room for anyone else in my heart.

"I quit."

"You can't quit," I cried. "You promised me that you'd—"

"I promised to keep you safe. To watch over you." He slashed his arm through the air. "I didn't promise to watch you suck face with an asshole like him."

I swallowed. "I don't even like him like that."

"I wish you the best of luck with life, but I can't do this anymore. I care about you too much to stay at the side, watching you move on. I just…can't."

And with that, he turned on his heel and disappeared.

I wrapped my arms around myself and blinked back tears. He was leaving, and I'd never see him again. I should be happy. Thrilled. Instead, I wanted to chase after him and beg him to stay.

CHAPTER TWENTY-FIVE

Finn

The next morning, my temper had cooled quite a bit, even if my feelings for Carrie hadn't. One thing I knew I had to do? I had to tell her I loved her before I left. I had to give it one last shot. If she told me she didn't give a damn about my feelings, then I'd leave. At least I would know I gave it all I had. I wouldn't spend my life wondering what would have happened if I'd gotten the balls to tell her I loved her.

I hadn't been lying when I told her yesterday she deserved better than me. She did. But no one else would love her as much as I could. No one else could make her feel as good, either. My phone rang and I glanced down. When I saw it was the senator, I sighed and picked it up. "Good morning, sir."

"What's this I hear about you punching Cory Pinkerton? What happened?"

I rubbed my temples. "Who told you?"

"The police called the campus, and the campus called me." The senator sighed. "I'll get it taken care of, but you better have a damned good reason for punching someone who could very well be a huge contributor to my campaign in the future."

I swallowed the curses wanting to escape. "Yeah. Because your *campaign* is the most important thing here."

"Are you insulting me, son?" His tone dropped, and I clenched the phone. "I can just as easily let the cops get their hands on your sorry ass. I'm sure your father would be displeased."

Minus a huge pension, no doubt.

"No, *sir*." I cleared my throat. "No disrespect."

"Good." I could practically hear the smug grin the senator wore. "Now tell me what happened."

I filled him in, but in my version of the story, Carrie had already left and my cover hadn't been blown. "So, I told him I was a jealous ex, punched him, and told him never to come near her again."

"I'll kill the little brat," the senator said. "How dare he act that way toward my girl?"

I clenched my jaw. "I felt the same way, sir."

"Good work, son. Keep in the shadows, and don't be seen."

This was the time to tell him I quit. Tell him I couldn't stay here anymore, but I hung up on him without another word and tossed my phone across the bed. I'd had to make up a story, so now I had to fill Carrie in on the tale I'd told. Time to track her down and fill her in. And while I was at it, I'd tell her I was in love with her too.

I'd leave after she laughed in my face.

Carrie

I lifted my hand to knock on Finn's door, but it swung open before I could. There he stood, looking breathtakingly gorgeous as always. I had spent an hour out on the water, enjoying the solitude of the ocean. Everyone out there seemed to be trying to escape something. I wanted to escape it all. My life. Cory. My father.

And most of all…Finn. He was leaving me.

I didn't even know how I felt about him anymore. I knew when Finn was around, my heart begged for me to forgive him. To give him another chance. But my head screamed just as loudly, and it called my heart a fool. How could I trust him after everything he'd done? After everything we'd been through?

I couldn't. That's how.

"Carrie? What are you doing here?"

I licked my lips and focused on him. I wasn't sure what I was going to say yet. I probably should have thought that through. "I'm checking in to see if you heard from my dad yet."

"He called. He was informed that Cory pressed charges against me."

I closed my eyes. I'd been up all night worrying about that. "I *told* you he would do that. We'll fix this. I'm sure if I speak to him, tell him who I really am, he'll—"

"No."

I stiffened. "Why not?"

"Because you're not blowing your cover for me."

"What if I want to?"

"I don't care." He lifted a brow. "Besides, your father's taking care of it. I had to fabricate a story so that he wouldn't know I was outed to you, but he bought it."

Wait, if he lied and didn't tell him about me knowing his identity, did that mean he was staying? *Please God, yes.* "What did you tell him?"

Finn quickly relayed the fabricated story, and I nodded. "That was quick thinking."

"No, it wasn't. I was up all night, waiting." He shrugged. "I couldn't sleep, anyway."

I looked up at him. "Me either."

Our gazes latched, and he turned a little bit red. "Look, Carrie, I—"

"Are you still leaving?" I asked at the same time.

He broke off. "Do you want me to?"

"I don't want you to," I said slowly, not dropping my gaze. "I want you to stay, but I get it if you can't."

"Can you ever forgive me? For lying?"

"I do forgive you." I took a deep breath. All night long, I'd been asking myself this very question. Asking myself if I could ever understand his motivation. It wasn't until I answered just now that I realized I already had. "I forgive you for it all. I understand why you did what you did."

His eyes lit up. "Do you think you can ever… Can we ever…?"

I wished I could say yes, but he'd hit me where I was weakest. All my life, Dad had been paying people to get close to me. And the first man I fell in love with was one of them. It hurt too much. Brought back too many memories—none of them good.

He made a choking sound. "You don't have to answer. I can see it in your eyes."

"I'm so sorry," my voice a mere whisper. It's all I could manage past my aching throat.

He swallowed hard. "I love you, will always love you. I'm sorry I killed us before we even had a chance."

And with that bombshell, he shut the door in my face.

CHAPTER TWENTY-SIX

Finn

Well, there you had it. I'd told her I loved her. Had asked for another chance. She'd said no. Chapter over. End of our story. I'd always known she was smart, and she'd proved it even more by rejecting me. She deserved more than I could give her. Security. Diamonds. A fucking mansion.

With another man, she could get all those things and more.

I slammed my fist into the wall, trembling from the force of the frustration and anger and pain storming through me. What had I been thinking, falling for her? What made me think I could find a way to make her forgive me, when I had so clearly fucked up? She didn't love me. She never would.

A knock sounded on the door, and I yanked it open. Carrie still stood there. "How dare you?"

I closed my fist around the knob, ignoring the way my heart leapt at the sight of her. "How dare I what?"

She shoved my shoulders, and I backed up. "You don't tell someone you love them and then just *leave*. What the hell is wrong with you?"

I rubbed where her hand had impacted with my shoulder and raised a brow. "You might as well sit if you want me to list everything. It could take all day."

"*Shut up*, you idiot. God, you make me so...so..." She made a frustrated sound and covered her face. "Mad."

I dropped my hand and held my breath. "Carrie?"

"Did you mean it?" She lifted her head, her eyes shooting a challenge at me I would gladly accept. Any day. Any time. Anywhere. "Do you really love me? Or are you just trying to trick me into thinking you do?"

I frowned at her. I wouldn't dignify that with a response. "What do you think?"

"*Finn.*" She advanced on me. "I need to know. I need to hear it."

I growled. With one quick step, I had her in my arms and I was kissing her. Kissing her so she would shut the hell up and stop shooting questions at me. Kissing her because if I didn't, I might die. When she stopped squirming in my arms, and instead clung to me, I broke off the kiss.

Cupping her cheeks, I met her eyes and said, "I want to be your man. To show you how happy I can make you. I promise you, with all my heart and soul, that I'm not lying about this. I'm not making anything up. Not anymore."

"Finn..."

"I'm falling in love with you, Ginger." I kissed her nose. "Hell, who am I kidding? I'm already there. I'm not exactly used to this feeling. If you want me to leave, then I'll go. You can fall for someone who is much more appropriate for you. If you want me to stay, I'll spend the rest of my life making you happy, or I'll die trying. Just say the word."

"My father's going to kill you," she said, tears falling out of her eyes. "Because I love you too."

My heart stuttered to a stop, then sped back up to light speed. Beam me up, fucking Scotty. She loved me. "You do?"

"I do." She kissed me gently, then shoved me back again. "But if you ever even *think* about lying to me again, I'll cut off your balls and shove them so far up your butt you won't even know they're missing. Got it?"

I laughed. "Got it."

My phone buzzed in my pocket, and she raised a brow. "Who is that?"

"Your father, no doubt." I twisted around to yank it out, holding it down so she could see. No more secrets. *Got the problem taken care of. Where is she now?* "Hm. I can't lie, so..." I picked her up and carried her to my bed, falling down on top of her. Then I texted, *She's still in bed.*

Carrie laughed when I showed her what I wrote. "Tell him I'm with three different men, but not to worry. They're all Ivy League."

I growled and nibbled at her throat. "No way. You're all mine."

"No arguments here. Not anymore." She clung to my shoulders and arched her throat to give me better access. "But he doesn't know it, and he can't."

I lifted my head. "Why don't you want to tell him? Is it because you don't want anyone to know about me? About us?"

"What? No. *No!*" She smoothed my hair off my face. "I don't want your father to lose his pension. He's always been kind to me, and I need to return the favor. After this year is over, and after your father is done, we'll tell my father together. Until then, we'll wait."

The fact that she cared enough about Dad's well-being to lie to her own father only made me fall for her even more. "Are you sure?"

"Positive as a proton."

I laughed and kissed her. My phone buzzed again, and I held it up so she could read. *You'll be returning home with her for winter break. Your father has requested you visit, so I arranged it all.*

Yes, sir.

I chucked the phone aside and settled in between her legs. "Looks like we'll be spending Christmas together, Ginger."

"Good." She trailed her fingers down my spine, then over my ass. "I can't go too long without this."

"You're going to have to if you want us to be a secret." I lowered my body, nibbling at her shoulder now. "Because when I make you come, you scream, babe."

"I do *not*," she said haughtily. "I never scream."

"Oh yeah?"

I ran my hand down her stomach, tracing the waistband of her shorts. "I just might have to prove you wrong…"

I closed my mouth over hers, and she slipped her tongue inside my mouth. I groaned in satisfaction, savoring her taste. Her smell. The way she moved underneath of me, undulating her body and asking for more. More that I'd readily give her. Anything she wanted. The moon. The stars. It would be hers.

She gripped my ass, yanking me against her. "God, I need you."

"Not nearly as much as I need you."

I kissed her gently before I took off her sweatshirt. I made quick work of her bra, and then closed my fingers around her bare breasts.

When I kneaded them and bit down on her shoulder, she cried out and dug her nails into my back. I hissed, half in pain and half in pleasure, and captured her mouth once more.

I rolled her nipples between my thumbs and fingers, tugging with just enough pressure to make her squirm. When she trembled and moaned into my mouth, I lowered my hands to her waist and yanked her shorts off. Once she was blessedly naked, I made quick work of my own shorts, then grabbed a condom and tossed it on the bed. I laid down on the bed and rolled her on top until she straddled my hips.

The sight of her perfect breasts hanging above me was almost too much to take in. I lifted my head and urged her down, closing my mouth around her nipple while gripping her hips with my hands. She let out a surprised cry and speared me with her nails, leaving little half-moon marks on my pecs.

She shoved my shoulders back and took a shaky breath. "That's enough of that. I want to explore this new position."

Her long hair cascaded around her breasts and her back, making her look wanton. Sexy. "You look so hot right now."

She looked down at me with smoky eyes and crawled down my body. When she nibbled on my abs, I flinched and buried my hands in her hair. Without hesitation, she closed her lips around me, sucking me in deep. I groaned and closed my eyes, letting her mouth move over me. Torture me. When she rolled her tongue over the head, I bit my tongue to keep from crying out. From begging her to stop…or to never stop.

I didn't know which need would win.

Reaching down, I picked her up and set her aside. After grabbing the foil and putting on a condom, I lowered her to my cock, spreading her legs wide. "I need you *now*."

She gripped my shaft and lowered herself onto me, inch by torturous inch. My balls tightened, and I practically came right there. I'd never been one to get carried away by passion, but with my Carrie…I didn't have a choice. She touched me, and I was gone.

I reached up and cupped her face, bringing her down for a slow, passionate kiss. She whimpered into my mouth and moved faster on me, trying to find a rhythm that would give her what she needed. What I needed too.

I ended the kiss. "Let me try something I think you'll enjoy." I tucked her legs behind her body, lifted her up, and then rocked my hips into hers. She shrieked, her nails digging into my skin. "You like that?"

"Again," she rasped, her perfect lips parted. "Do it again."

I lifted her up a little bit, then lowered her body as I lifted my own, and she cried out. I grinned. "See? Told you you were too loud."

"Just shut up and do it again," she said, ending on a plea.

I did it again. And again. By the time I reached the third thrust, we were both too lost to talk anymore, let alone think. When her tight muscles clenched down on my cock, warning me of her impending orgasm, my own pleasure grew to a pinnacle. With one last thrust, we both exploded and sank into the mattress, her sweaty body resting against my equally damp one.

I ran my fingers over her back and smoothed her hair over her face. She cuddled in closer, letting out a contented sigh. "Yeah, I can't live without that."

I chuckled. "I don't think I can either. We'll find a way to keep you quiet."

"Me?" She reared back and glowered at me, but the sparkle in her eye ruined the effect she was going for. "I think we need to worry about you, not me."

I hugged her close. "I have no idea what you're talking about."

She climbed off me and headed for the bathroom. "I'm going to go in here for a minute, and then you're going to cook for me."

"Is that all you want me for?" I rolled onto my stomach and grinned. "Food and sex?"

Her head poked out of the bathroom. "And booze."

"Brat," I called out.

She shut the door in my face and I laughed. When I stood up, I stretched my arms high over my head and made my way to the trash can to get rid of the condom. I couldn't believe she'd forgiven me. Given me a chance to prove to her how much I could be trusted. Life couldn't get any better than this.

After I stepped into my shorts, I heard my phone buzz. Padding across the room, I bent down and picked it up. I'd apparently missed a call earlier, and had a voicemail notification. When I recognized the number, I sank onto the bed and swallowed hard. This couldn't be good news. I just knew it. Could *feel* it in my gut.

I hit the *play message* button, then listened to the brief but life-changing message. When it ended, I let my hand fall to my side. Fuck. This wasn't going to be good, and it was going to make Carrie cry. I didn't want to make her cry ever again.

But I couldn't hide the truth from her. Not again.

The door opened and she came out wearing my favorite red shirt. The same one she'd worn twice already. I tossed my phone aside and plastered on a smile. "Damn, babe, you look better in that than I do."

"You think?" She posed in the doorway, bending one perfect leg and shooting me a *come get me* smile. "I might just keep it. It smells like you."

I stood up and swept her into my arms, hugging her as tightly as I could. "If you want it, it's yours. Anything you want."

"Well, then." She lifted her face and smiled up at me, her eyes shining with tears. Happy tears. "All I want is you."

I swallowed hard. "You got me."

"I did," she whispered, rising up on tiptoes and kissing me. "And now you need to *feed* me."

She skipped toward the kitchen, and I followed her with a smile. After dinner, I would fill her in. Give her the news. But we could be blissfully happy for a few hours, right? Because right now, I was too busy being fucking happy that I'd gotten the girl of my dreams. The girl I loved, and who also loved me.

Imagine that.

Watch for book two in 2014

ACKNOWLEDGEMENTS

First and foremost, I'd like to thank my family. I crammed in the time to write this book for Carrie and Finn, but in turn, my family got to see me hunched over my desk as I did so. Thank you for your love and understanding. Without your support, I'd never have gotten this done.

To my agent, Louise Fury, and her wonderful pit crew, thank you so much for your advice and editing help! And all your guidance and advice and the support. Oh my God, the support! You are all like magical unicorns in the publishing world. You're the bee's knees, and I heart you all.

To my wonderful publicist with InkSlinger PR, Jessica Estrep, thank you for all the unwavering support and dedication you gave to this book and to me. I'm so, so happy I signed with InkSlinger PR, and even happier I got you!

To Heidi McLaughlin and Caisey Quinn, thank you for listening to me panic, whine, bitch, and moan as I learned the ropes of this crazy new adult world. And thanks for all the tips, pointers, and help, too. You two are the best friends a girl could ask for! Lots of hugs and kisses!

To my beta readers, thank you! You all gave me invaluable advice and support, and you helped shape *Out of Line* into what it is today. I'll be sure to send book two your way once I, you know, write it.

To Casey Harris-Parks, Jessica Estep, Louise Fury, and all of her pit crew—thank you for the hours and hours and hours spent deliberating over the perfect title for Finn and Carrie. I couldn't have done it without you! Seriously!

And to all of the readers out there, keep on reading.

ABOUT THE AUTHOR

Jen McLaughlin writes steamy New Adult books for the young and young at heart. Her first release came out September 2013. She also writes Contemporary Romance under the pen name Diane Alberts. She is a multi-published, bestselling author and is represented by Louise Fury from the L. Perkins Agency. Since receiving her first contract offer under the pen name Diane Alberts, she has yet to stop writing.

Though she lives in the mountains, she really wishes she was surrounded by a hot, sunny beach with crystal clear water. She lives in Northeast Pennsylvania with her four kids, a husband, a schnauzer mutt, a cat, and a Senegal parrot. In the rare moments when she's not writing, she can usually be found hunched over one knitting project or another. Her goal is too write so many well-crafted romance books that even a non-romance reader will know her name.

CPSIA information can be obtained at www.ICGtesting.com
Printed in the USA
LVOW08s1544151013

357040LV00003B/665/P

9 780989 668408

[9]